SHADOW

Educated in the US a.. ..K, Philip Brebner received a PhD from Glasgow University for his thesis on architecture and urban design in Algeria 1830-1982. After lecturing at architecture schools in Jeddah and Porto, his first novel, *A Country of Vanished Dreams,* was published by Picador to critical acclaim, and translated. As well as fiction, he has published in academic journals and the Independent. To keep the wolves from the door, he taught creative writing for the British Council and dealt in rare rugs and textiles in Istanbul. He now divides his time between Portugal and Morocco, the inspiration for *Shadows of Marrakech.* The next novel in the series will be *Shadows of Essaouira.*

By the same author

A COUNTRY OF VANISHED DREAMS

THE FABULOUS ROAD

LIGHTER THAN AIR

FADO

Author website: www.philipbrebner.com

First published 2013 by Thames Street Press, Oxford

Copyright © Philip Brebner 2013

ISBN: 978-1-9196075-1-1

With thanks to my agents Andrew Kidd and the late Gillon Aitken.

Cover illustration by: www.andyfielding.co.uk

Design: www.lrbcreative.com

To Maria João, Philipa and Leonora,

with love

SHADOWS OF MARRAKECH

Philip Brebner

THAMES STREET PRESS

OXFORD

SHADOWS OF MARRAKECH

ONE

Near where Ramzi lived in Marrakech stood a neglected house with an old well that people were forbidden to open. According to legend a jinnee built it for the Black Sultan, who gave it to a holy saint, Sidi Mohammed ben Azouz, to use as a shrine for his cult. The saint knew the Sultan wanted to make mischief, and the jinnee still dwelt in the property, but he accepted the gift. Arriving with the keys, a slave welcomed him. In reply, the saint chanted an incantation, and the slave changed into the jinnee and fled inside. The saint chased it to the well, and the jinnee jumped in to escape. Smart as a whip, the saint blocked up the well and barricaded the doorway, but as he left the jinnee put a curse on the saint's family to prevent them from ever inhabiting the house, or using it as a shrine, or putting in a fountain, or digging a new well.

The house, many centuries old, fell into

disrepair. Yet it had such a magical reputation that the pretender to the Moroccan sultanate, Al Hiba, sent his soldiers to take possession of it in 1912 and make an ally of the jinnee imprisoned in the well. But a month later the French colonial power thrashed both Al Hiba and his resistance movement. Ramzi suspected he might have stopped believing in jinn after that.

Once, Ramzi was skeptical of jinn. Lately, after what happened to Nicole, every time he passed the passageway leading to the house, he recalled that tale, and wondered—was it really superstition?

The house stood near the shrine of Sidi Bel Abbes in a residential quarter in the north of the medina, Marrakech's historic walled city. But these were not houses in the Western sense. Their rooms were built around a courtyard. If planted with a tree it was called a 'riad', and if not, a 'dar'. Beyond the studded front doors every riad or dar was unique. There were small palaces with courtyards planted with citrus or pomegranate trees and jasmine and bougainvillea. There were modest abodes and tragic hovels. All looking inward, it was rare to find a window onto the street, and built cheek-by-jowl, it made it hard to mark one from the other. As for the dusty lanes, they swerved and swung, leaving a stranger disorientated. Some alleyways were too tight to fit a donkey with panniers, others collapsed into tunnels. And there always existed the fear of an abrupt dead-end.

Ramzi bought his riad from a couple whose North African dream turned into a nightmare. He overheard them playing the blame game at the next table in a restaurant where he was dining alone.

'It's because you kept changing the layout of the bathrooms that we ended up with hot-flushing toilets—'

'And who kept hacking away at the kitchen so it fitted an American fridge? And made the wall smash into the neighbours' salon during their son's gala circumcision? The Iman had such a fright, the scalpel slipped and the boy nearly lost the lot.'

'Yeah, all for the fridge we couldn't afford. Which is hardly a surprise after you had the roof terrace retiled because you wanted herringbone rather than hexagons—'

Interrupting, Ramzi struck up a conversation. First thing next morning they showed him the property. It dated back to 1760. The street level had risen since the house was built, so once inside he needed to descend a few metres to the courtyard. In the classic style, four orange trees framed a fountain. On one wall, giving to the salon, towered a double door the height of two men and hand carved with Islamic geometries painted in subdued colours; even in the museums of Marrakech it would be hard to find a door of equal quality. Two other rooms gave to the courtyard but their cedar doors were plain and opened to make entrances like keyholes. Octagonal columns reached up from the courtyard to support galleries that provided access to the upper rooms. The price was right, the papers in order, and the place became his.

Thereupon, he met Hisham. Paid by the previous owners as the riad's caretaker, the sleek, bright-eyed young man had a degree in economics, but professional jobs were few and far between. On the morning Ramzi picked up the keys, Hisham appeared dressed in a white shirt, black trousers and polished shoes, and presented a single page c.v.

'I am applying for the position of riad manager. There are the renovations to finish, and as you intend to run it as a guest house—'

'But I thought I'd be the manager?'

Hisham asked Ramzi if knew a reliable

builder? Did he know how to register the riad with the chamber of commerce and the tourist board? Hisham reeled off a list of chores: collecting clients from the airport, making restaurant reservations and organizing trips, arranging repairs, shopping for essentials, out-sourcing laundry, paying bills—

'Enough! When can you start?'

'I already have. The builder's waiting outside.'

Within hours Hisham started to work on a website, phoned a friend at a travel agency, conjured up a housekeeper, Latifa, and put Ramzi in touch with an accountant, Abdelfattah.

At last the day came when Ramzi laid out his collection of rare rugs and kilims on the sand-coloured floors of the white rooms, and adjusted the furniture. Outside, Hisham screwed a brass plate on the front door: *Riad Waqi*.

They were in business.

TWO

Unlike Yuletide, January in Marrakech was a quiet month for tourists. A young Frenchman, Paul Gallisot, was the only guest, and he cut rather a sad figure as he ate breakfast alone on the roof terrace.

After initial formalities, Ramzi kept out of Paul's way until, on the third day, he found Hisham striding up and down the courtyard. Paul had greeted him that morning with his customary '*Bonjour!*' but he had pronounced the word with what could only be described as bloated 'o's.

'Yesterday our guest upset Latifa, and now he's making fun of my French,' Hisham said. Ramzi assured Hisham he must be mistaken: his French, like most educated Moroccans, was fluent. Still, Ramzi decided to go and have a diplomatic word.

To his surprise, Paul greeted him with the same round 'o's. Despite Paul's young age, twenty-seven according to his passport, Ramzi wondered if this strange pronunciation might be the tell-tale sign of a stroke. But as Paul continued, Ramzi realized his French slipped into a type of dialect. He said he'd forgotten to ask Hisham if he could arrange a trip up to the Ourika Valley. Picturesque and set deep in the High Atlas, the excursion always proved a hit with visitors, and Ramzi promised to arrange a *grand* taxi for the following morning.

'*Merci, ti'es très aimabe.*'

Those were his exact words. Yet, when he met Paul three days ago, the young man had spoken educated French. Now it sounded less nasal, more guttural like Arabic. He no longer addressed Ramzi as *vous* but informally, as *tu,* and pronounced *ti'es* instead of *tu es.* And the 'l' in *aimable* had been annihilated.

The afternoon before Paul was due to return to France, Ramzi paid a routine visit to the accountant in Guéliz, the new town built outside the medina walls. The office was on the third floor of a block built in colonial times, the sign FIDUCIAIRE ABDELFATTAH fixed beside an air conditioner cantilevered over the street.

There was no lift, just grey stairs that led to a tidy office with a picture of the Holy Mosque in Makkah on the wall. The window revealed the tops of trees sprinkled with spring buds and beyond them a cinema, Le Colisée. After shaking hands Abdelfattah sat behind the desk and made a long play of polishing his glasses, before opening the Riad Waqi file, and launching into a diatribe.

Tax dodges, tax breaks, social security payments, Ramzi found it bewildering.

'And that brings me to the case of the missing bank statements.'

'A mystery: that's just what I need.'

'This is a serious matter, Monsieur Ramzi. If a man puts a cord around his neck, God will provide someone to pull it.'

'So how do I duck the executioner?'

'Visit the bank and ask for copies. And be careful to check they've been stamped.' Another sermon followed. Enlightened, if not uplifted, Ramzi wrote the quarterly cheque.

'Good: no mistakes this time,' Abdelfattah said and opened a pot on his desk. 'Take a sweet before you leave.'

The taste of tamarind still in his mouth, Ramzi reached Bab Doukkala, the majestic gateway to the west of the medina. A plump daymoon shone in the fading sky and a thin wind swirled dust into his throat. Crossing the plaza by the bus station, he reached the ramparts. The old city walls stood high and pink and were fronted by kiosks selling second-hand books and magazines, for the most part in Arabic and French.

He picked up a chemistry textbook for the Moroccan Baccalauréat, scanning the section on atoms, molecules and ions. Since his first chemistry set, a Christmas present from his Scottish grandmother, Ramzi was seduced by the wizardry of colour changes and bangs, by the tubes filled with exotic names, and by the fascination of growing crystals. As a child for whom curiosity was a compulsion, chemistry answered this need. Growing older he'd studied the interaction of matter and materials in the world around him, and enjoyed the maths and logic it demanded. At university, he discovered a talent for mixing imagination and intuition with calculations and reasoning. But nowadays he missed the intellectual challenge.

Replacing the book, he absent-mindedly picked up a paperback on North London murders.

'How much?'

'Pay what you like—'

'What? OK. Seven Yen—'

'This is Marrakech, not Tokyo.'

'Fine, give me the Moroccan price.'

'Ten dirhams—'

'That's daylight robbery. All these pages are dog-eared and the spine's broken. Look, this chapter on Dr Crippen is hanging by a thread. Two dirhams.'

'You are a like a Berber, monsieur. But listen my grandmother is old—'

'So is mine—'

This time the vendor laughed. Price agreed, money exchanged hands as the call to prayer soared over the city. Continuing home Ramzi felt the cold cascade as the sky darkened and the sun turned blood red. The ramparts faded, smoke billowed from the charcoal fire of a kebab stall, men rose and fell on prayer mats in a roped-off zone, and ahead the feathered leaves of a palm grove shivered in the breeze. At the curb-side a Mercedes taxi pulled up. A family piled out with suitcases, bags, boxes bound with string. Opening the boot, they hauled out a sheep with its forelegs fettered.

Ramzi sidestepped the poor animal. *Eid al-Adha*, a fortnight away, celebrated Abraham's willingness to sacrifice his son Ishmael for God. But as the knife hovered God commanded a sheep to be offered up instead. To commemorate this, every year most Muslim families slaughtered a sheep of their own, dividing the meat between family, friends and the poor. Already holiday fever seized Marrakech, though privately Ramzi couldn't wait till it was all over.

Veering right through a small gateway in the ramparts, he zigzagged along a slim passageway that opened into a wider lane. Reaching his door, he fumbled for the key. As he did so he saw a man in the shadows. In this cul-de-sac it was unusual for men to loiter, and Ramzi hoped it wasn't becoming a venue for drug dealers. Sighing, he slid the key into the lock and gave it a quarter turn anti-clockwise.

THREE

Inside, lights set in little alcoves picked out the stairs that led the way down to the courtyard. Ramzi liked to maintain standards, even when he had only a single guest. In the kitchen, he found a box of matches and crouched down to light a tea-candle in the iron lanterns, one under each orange tree. Flickering flames and the scent of jasmine gathered with the night to give a sense of security and shelter. Back in the kitchen, he wiped the dust off the covers of the paperback he had bought and twisted a corkscrew into a bottle of Meknes *Beni M'tir* red wine, but the cork broke as he pulled it out. Cursing, he carefully ran a finger round the inside of the neck to slide out the bits.

'*Bonsoir.*'

The bottle toppled; a hand saved it, and put it upright. The way those 'o's beefed-up *bonsoir*, the dexterous stranger had to be Paul Gallisot.

Ramzi thanked him and wondered where he

had come from. No thud betrayed a door; no light splashed the courtyard. Maybe he had been sitting in the dark. They both shook hands, but his guest's grip lacked verve.

Paul wanted to find Hisham to book a taxi to the airport at nine o'clock next morning. Hisham had the afternoon off, so Ramzi made a note of it. Recalling Paul's visit to the Ourika Valley, Ramzi snapped into hospitality mode and feigned interest in the trip.

But Paul's reply was curt, so much so that Ramzi found himself offering the guest a drink to mask his astonishment. Paul accepted, and Ramzi led him past the orange trees and the fountain towards the salon and showed him to one of the banquette sofas lining the walls. At one end, twisted logs lay in the hearth of a fireplace. Ramzi knelt in front of the mantelpiece, and with a couple of firelighters and a few puffs of the bellows, the wood crackled into life. He poured two glasses of wine, annoyed at a piece of rogue cork floating in his glass.

'People never think winter nights in Morocco can be cold. I like the tiles. Is it something from the Qur'an?'

Paul referred to the panel of Arabic

calligraphy running above the hearth. Ramzi explained it was a proverb, as it wouldn't be decorous drinking wine in front of a verse from the Qur'an. The tiles read: *The weight of the burden is known only by he who carries it.*

Paul nodded, and gulped back the Meknes rouge. For a moment he looked preoccupied, and Ramzi thought he saw tears well up in the young man's eyes. But Paul recovered himself.

'How long have you had the riad?'

'About a year.'

'And are things going well?'

'They're picking up. The suicide bombings in Casablanca last May didn't help. Lots of tourists panicked and cancelled, as one might expect.'

Ramzi recalled the photograph of the targeted restaurant, the Casa de Espanhà. Upturned chairs, abandoned paella dishes, scattered cutlery, broken plates, glasses and bottles of wine. Maybe Paul was remembering it too, because again he looked lost in a painful dream.

'So, do you like Morocco?' Ramzi asked, pretending he hadn't noticed.

'Once upon a time, I used to work here.'

'And you're back here on business?'

'No. I missed Marrakech. I went to see where I used to live, and—and I wanted to buy a kilim.'

For some reason Ramzi doubted this.

'What type of kilim did you buy?' Paul pointed to the floor.

'It's like this one.'

Well he knew a kilim from a rug. But this particular piece came from the Caucasus on the periphery of Turkey and Russia. Not everyone was a connoisseur, and Ramzi had no reason to disbelieve him, but something about Paul's manner prompted him to find out more. He asked Paul where he had lived in Marrakech.

'I had an apartment behind the Majorelle Garden. About a fifteen-minute walk from here. That's why I picked your riad, because it was close. I'd have preferred to live in the medina, but the apartment had a great view and was more anonymous. No one batted an eyelid—not even the concierge—when I came or went, or arrived from the hypermarket with bags of clinking wine bottles. Don't you find that a problem here with the neighbours?'

'We have the wine delivered.' Paul settled back against the cushions.

'Yes, I suppose so. Of course, what makes

Moroccan cities like Marrakech and Fes so magical is the contrast between the old city and the new city. We have to thank Marshal Lyautey and the French Protectorate for that. The way he preserved the old buildings and traditional society in the imperial capitals by building the colonial city outside the medina walls was a master-stroke.'

For a minute Ramzi half-expected him to break into the Marseillaise.

'Some historians see this division into a "Moroccan" quarter and a "European" quarter as a form of apartheid.'

'And if the French had moved into the medina en masse they would have been called vandals. Anyhow, I'll always love Algeria more than Morocco. That country is in my blood. My mother's family lived there till Independence in 1962. Afterwards she married and returned with my father. He was a petrochemical engineer. I spent my childhood there. But we left when the civil war broke out.'

Hearing this, Ramzi smiled to himself. So, he'd been right about Paul's mercurial accent: the patois originated from his family's colonial background. He reached for the wine to offer another glass, but Paul glanced at his gold and steel Rolex.

'Thanks for the wine. I'd like to talk some more, but as it's my last night I want to make the most of it.'

Ramzi refilled his own glass and stood to say goodbye. As they shook hands he noticed something surprising about Paul's expression, a sense of excitement.

At the door, he turned, reminding Ramzi that his passport was in the office safe.

'I'll get it—'

'No, it's better not. I'll collect it after breakfast. I'll see you then.'

Sitting back down, Ramzi heard his guest climb the stairs and walk along the gallery. Light gilded the courtyard. After a few minutes, the bolt smacked shut on the bedroom door. The entrance clicked. He was gone.

A pall of silence fell over the riad. Ramzi retrieved the paperback. After tossing another couple of logs on the fire, he started reading. He skipped the exploits of Jack the Ripper, because *Eid al-Adha* brought throat cutting enough. Instead he read the cases of Ruth Ellis, who shot her boyfriend after a series of violent arguments, and Kenneth Halliwell, who became inflamed with jealousy after reading the diary of his lover, the playwright Joe Orton, and killed him with nine blows of a hammer, before taking an overdose of barbiturates.

Ramzi shivered as the fire died away. Collecting the wineglasses and bottle he crossed between the orange trees. Stars studded the heavens; wood smoke softened the air. In the kitchen, he rinsed out the glasses, setting them on the drainer. Unlocking the office, he phoned to arrange the nine o'clock taxi to the airport and for want of anything better to do, opted to go to bed.

At the corner of the courtyard a narrow archway opened to a separate staircase. It led to the *douriya*, a small apartment in the riad, traditionally used by the eldest son of the family, but now his own private domain. The stairs needed concentration, as the risers were irregular. Opening the door, he dumped the book on the sill of one the three windows overlooking the courtyard. Changing out of his clothes he walked barefoot across the Afghan rug to the double bed.

He flinched as he slid beneath the cold covers. His mind ran over the talk with Paul and the similarities between them, a foot in North Africa, a foot in Europe. But the parallel was skewed. Part of him was Moroccan. Paul was a Frenchman. They were not the same.

FOUR

Even in winter Ramzi left the window by the bed ajar to hear the *fijar*, or summons to dawn prayer, though in fact it came earlier, at false-dawn. The local muezzin was young and blessed with a honeyed voice and his call poured into the alleys and courtyards. Normally Ramzi drifted back to sleep when it ended, but that night his mind churned over his conversation with Paul and acidified into memories of his final year in Britain.

First, an elderly woman had started hitting him with her umbrella at a bus stop, accusing him of singlehandedly felling the Twin Towers in New York and causing the woes of the world.

'Go back to your own country!'

'To Scotland?' he said, but this prompted another beating for impudence.

Ramzi might have dismissed this as either foolishness or dementia and laughed it off. Shortly afterwards, walking home one evening across the university campus, a group of students called him 'a half-caste' and as he walked on an empty beer can hit him square in the back.

The two incidents started a chain reaction. As Ramzi watched TV or read the press he could no longer shrug off the way Muslims were demonized, and Islam was portrayed as dangerous and irrational. Increasingly he felt trepidation and disquiet.

Over lunch, he mentioned this to a Jewish friend, who replied, 'I don't blame you. If these headlines substituted "Jew" for "Muslim" I'd not only feel scared, but I'd grab my passport and run.'

'Where would I run to?'

'You've lived in Britain nearly all your life. Put your career on hold and go to Morocco. After all, it is your maternal country. Who knows what might happen when you're there?'

FIVE

Alarm clocks were redundant at Riad Waqi. Every morning, when the housekeeper Latifa arrived, she slammed the front door. The tremors shot through the walls and furniture with the force of a mortar attack. She came from a large family, and liked to find ways of making her presence felt.

Ramzi lay for a few minutes imagining his day. Breakfast, a merry *au revoir* to Paul Gallisot, hello to a party of English guests late afternoon plus a spiel on tackling Marrakech, empty hours in between. With a groan, Ramzi threw back the duvet, his blood thick with boredom.

Opening the window, a house bunting flew off the sill into an orange tree. Rubbing his bare arms against the sharp air, Ramzi headed to shower and dress, then made his way down the brick staircase, to the courtyard. Looking up, a square of blue was trimmed by the green pantiles that crowned the walls.

The smell of coffee wafted from the kitchen.

'*Bonjour* Monsieur Ramzi.'

'*Bonjour* Latifa.'

Latifa bustled round the kitchen. Her work clothes, the black embroidered tunic and trousers, emphasized her sturdiness, whilst a white headscarf struggled to conceal her hair.

A juice extractor whined as she rammed down another half orange. Ramzi drank his coffee black, a pure Arabica blended with cardamom and black pepper, no sugar. Usually, it kick-started the mornings. But the coffee he tasted today—it was an act of treachery!

'My God! What's this?'

'Hisham bought it. He said it saves us twenty dirhams per kilogram.'

Ramzi had agreed to a profit sharing arrangement with Hisham. Now he saw the idea starting to backfire. With the patience of Job, he trudged up to the roof terrace. Leaning against a table he gazed across a disarray of minarets, flat roofs, satellite discs and supernal palms. Against the walls, small olive trees, pink oleander, red hibiscus and purple bougainvillea burst from terracotta pots. Splashing the coffee around a bunny-eared cactus—

he hoped it lived—he patrolled the plants, picking out weeds.

Under the white canvas tent, he arranged the butterfly chairs. Noticing one of the four wooden tent-poles askew, he adjusted the guys. Secured against the parapet of the courtyard, he squatted down to tighten it. Standing up, he looked down at Paul Gallisot's room. Behind the decorative ironwork on the windows, the shutters were closed.

He checked his watch. Eight thirty. Paul's plane took off around eleven. Ramzi hurried downstairs. On a circular brass tray Latifa had organized orange juice, jam, yoghurt, a pot of coffee and milk and a basket of bread for their guest. When she added a pancake *galette*, Ramzi sighed. Not one of her strong points, it would be tough as boot leather.

Tray in hand, Ramzi arrived at the double door of Paul's room and discovered the outside bolt still in the lock. Perhaps Paul had mistaken the time of his flight, and left early. Ramzi tried to remember if he'd paid. He deposited the tray, shot the bolt back, and swung open one of the cedar doors.

'Monsieur Gallisot?'

The interior was empty and the bed untouched. Yanking the window shutters, sunlight and arabesque shadows from the ironwork flooded the surfaces. To poke around a guest's room was taboo, but Ramzi felt he had no choice. The Delsey suitcase lay open, unpacked. In a niche serving as a nightstand, lay an e-ticket. The flight departed at 10.20, in less than two hours. With border queues, fantastic fun. He spotted a slight lump in the white duvet. Running a hand underneath, he found Paul's Rolex watch, mobile phone and wallet.

He guessed Paul had hidden his phone and valuables because he knew his plans for a night out carried risks. Ramzi crossed to the bathroom. The towel and soap were dry. From beneath the sink he pulled out the bin. Inside were threads of dental floss and an empty bottle of *Sidi Ali* water.

'Monsieur Ramzi?'

Startled, he turned to face Hisham, ready to explain himself. But Hisham had other worries: he'd forgotten that the three couples arriving together that afternoon had requested dinner. In turn, Latifa had plans to pick up a prescription for her mother who suffered from Parkinson's disease. The doctor's surgery lay on the other side of the medina, and Latifa loved to dawdle. This could leave little time to shop and cook dinner for six.

Ramzi would have to collect the prescription. If Paul still hadn't turned up he'd stop on the way to report his disappearance to the Tourist Police.

'Who'll break the news to Latifa?'

'You're the manager—'

'You're the owner—' Hisham said.

'We'll both go.'

Downstairs, Latifa was chatting on the phone.

'We're sunk,' said Hisham. 'She's talking to her sister in Casablanca.'

'Latifa—'

'Hold on, it's the boss and his sidekick. Look, please be quick. Both of you know my sister is pregnant.'

Ramzi and Hisham glanced at each other. Who was the boss and who the sidekick?

Ding-dong!

'Hisham will explain.' Ramzi beat a retreat and opened the front door to Adbelsadak, the taxi driver who'd driven Paul to the Atlas Mountains. Apologizing, Ramzi explained the situation and offered to pay anyway but Abdelsadak refused.

'I'll wait. There's still time for him to make the flight.'

Ramzi led Abdelsadak to a table in the

courtyard, offering him coffee.

'No thank you.' He turned towards the kitchen. 'What's all that commotion? It sounds like a frying pan thrown at somebody.'

Ramzi switched subject. 'Did Paul enjoy his trip to the Ourika Valley? He seemed reluctant to talk about it.'

'Well, now you mention it, there was something puzzling.'

'What do you mean?'

'When we arrived, he had no interest in seeing the cataracts. I kept telling him how spectacular they are, but all he wanted was to go to Setti Fatma, the village nearby.'

'For any special reason?'

'He was searching for a woman. Someone called Zahra Ait El Amri. He asked me to help. People knew her, and we were sent up the hill to a small house. Yet when we reached the door, Monsieur Paul told me to go away. I thought I'd have to wait but he arrived at the taxi about ten minutes later and asked me to drive him straight back to Marrakech.'

SIX

'It's after 10.30.'

'A promise is a cloud, fulfilment is rain,' Abdelsadek said. 'See you!'

With still no sign of Paul, went to report the disappearance to the Tourist Police. As he walked, he thought over Abdelsadek's story, wondering if Paul had a romantic involvement with the woman he had searched for. Had he come to Marrakech to see her, only to have his hopes dashed? That would explain why he cut Ramzi short when he asked about his trip to the Ourika Valley.

Ramzi passed the shrine of Sidi Abdul Aziz, where a woman fastened a padlock to the ironwork window masking the saint's tomb. The gesture expected to attract baraka, *divine blessing*, to protect against an illness. It reminded Ramzi about Latifa's prescription. He hurried on to the soul of Marrakech, the open square, Djemma el-Fna, once the site of grisly executions. It had nothing regular or formal or grand about it; rather it resembled an encampment that had become permanent, the random buildings kneeling before the tall, straight-cut minaret of the Koutoubia Mosque standing on the periphery.

Now, with the snowy peaks of the Atlas as a backdrop, Djemma el-Fna had the excitement of a stage prepared for a performance. Although too soon in the day for the storytellers and acrobats, pounding drums clashed with snake charmers' pipes, creating a tension Ramzi found sinister.

Skirting the orange juice stalls, he reached the police station. Morocco has several branches of the police: Traffic Police, the Royal Guard, the Police Judiciaire, responsible for criminal justice, and the Tourist Police, the building where Ramzi now stood. He phoned Hisham. Paul Gallisot had still to return. Entering the station, Ramzi reported the 'no show.' The policeman took down the details: slim, about 1.78m, brown hair, light brown eyes, clean-shaven, French.

Duty done, he meandered towards the Café de France, avoiding the henna-tattooists perched on stools, pattern books and syringes at the ready. Leaving the square, he dodged scooters, bikes, and a flock of sheep, until he swerved right into Derb Djedid. Numbers ran sequentially, down one side and up the other, not like the west, odd opposite even. Several alleys branched off it, and on one corner three hucksters, average age six, sold bundles of grass, last meals for the sheep awaiting execution at *Eid*. Ramzi found 53 further along, and hammered a brass knocker, representing the hand of Fatima, the Prophet's daughter. A receptionist opened the door and asked him to wait in a room off a small courtyard. Steel and plastic chairs fringed a low table scattered with Moroccan and French periodicals, TelQel, Maroc Hebdo, Le Point, Paris Match. Two patients were in front of him, both women, and they exchanged glances with each other.

'Are you here to see Dr Rashida?'

'Yes.'

'You know she's a woman?'

'Women are excellent doctors.'

'Well you won't be disappointed. She's done wonders for my rheumatism. She wrote a magic formula on a large piece of paper with a special pen, asked me to fast for three days and then to soak the paper in water until it absorbed the ink. On the fourth day I drank the water, and afterwards put a few drops of oil in a bowl to mix with the rest of the ink and wiped it with the paper talisman. Then I rubbed it over my joints and in no time, they stopped aching.'

'What a happy coincidence,' Ramzi said. Snake oil!

'No, you're wrong. Tell him about your son.'

'My youngest son Idriss had pinkeye. Dr Rashida put a necklace with five pebbles round his neck as an amulet. After three days, I followed the instructions to remove the necklace and leave it in a busy place. I left it in Derb Dabachi—it's hard to find somewhere busier than that! And it was just as she said: the first person that looked at it snatched away the evil. As for my son's pinkeye: well, it vanished in a trice.'

'But—'

'Monsieur Ramzi?'

'Umm, there's no rush. I think I'm skipping the queue.'

The women waved him ahead with indulgent smiles. Inside the surgery, Ramzi half-expected to find a cauldron, jars of lurid potions and buckets of toads. Instead it contained a doctor's couch, an examination light, a screen, sink, sterilizer, fridge and scales, and on the wall, behind a desk, a framed diploma from the University of Rennes in France. The holder of the degree was less of a comedown. Braced for an old hag adorned with warts and claw-like fingernails, he encountered a radiant young woman, who greeted him with a charismatic smile and introduced herself as Dr Rashida. Her hair was uncovered but tied back. She wore a white coat over stonewashed jeans, and a stethoscope graced her neck.

Ramzi explained his mission on behalf of Latifa. Deadpan, he enquired if the prescription meant painting Latifa's mother with egg whites and tying a polka-dot ribbon in her hair, but immediately regretted his words.

'Are you calling me a charlatan?'

Ramzi blushed. 'I've just been hearing about your remedies for rheumatism and pinkeye.'

With a light laugh, she asked him to sit across from her desk, and tapped something into her laptop. As she closed it, he noticed she wore a wedding ring.

'I was born and raised in the medina. When I returned from France with my degree, I could have opened a swanky surgery in Guéliz. But it seemed more natural to set up here. It made me accessible, and I could help all sorts of poor people who in other circumstances might avoid going to a doctor. Not just because of cost, but because many still have no knowledge of medical science and were brought up with strong beliefs in folklore. Illness for many Moroccans has a magical or diabolical origin. Rather than fight it, I use each to the profit of the other. Whilst I practice modern medicine, if it suits the patient, I recommend a traditional remedy hand in hand.'

Ramzi felt foolish. 'I do apologize. It sounds like you know exactly what you're doing.'

He passed her Latifa's mother's identity card. Dr Rashida scribbled the prescription, and handed it to him with a smile.

'There, this is for a combination of carbidopa and levodopa. Plus, some vitamins.'

Thanking her, he stood up. At the door she said, 'By the way, you can get the polka-dot ribbon in the Rue Semarrine, and ninety-nine egg whites should do the trick.'

'For sure they will. "To God belong ninety-nine names."'

'I am impressed. You know something of Islam and its affinity for numbers. What about the anecdote? Who alone knows the hundredth name, the hidden name, the Greatest Name of all?'

'The camel with his mysterious smile.'

'Bravo! Now take a bow.'

Blushing again, Ramzi fled. But in the lane, he

almost turned back. His heart raced and he felt feverish. Even though she was married, a part of him felt dismayed he'd never see Dr Rashida again. But then he had no inkling how matters would unfold.

SEVEN

'*Bonjour.*'

    '*Guten Morgen, Fräulein.*'

    'Lovely jubbly.'

    'Feesh and cheeps.'

    '*Olé!*'

The tumult in the souks drowned out the call to *salat idh-dhuhr*, the noon prayer. It would soon be too late to collect the drugs for Latifa's mother. Walking faster Ramzi put the main bazaar behind him. Ahead a green crescent sign and the word PHARMARCIE ran vertically down the side of a building.

Still recovering from the cost of the Sinemet, he came into sight of Bab Taghzout, the old gateway. Dwarfing everything was the minaret and pyramidal emerald roof of the shrine of Sidi Bel Abbes, patron saint of Marrakech and the blind. In the courtyard, amputees in wheelchairs and sightless men and women asked for alms, and he dropped a few dirhams into outstretched hands at random. An elderly man in dark glasses tapped a white cane as a teenage boy guided him to join a group of the unseeing, sat shoulder-to-shoulder in an alcove, chanting verses from the Qur'an.

As he left the complex, a moped sputtered to a stop alongside him. The rider sported a crimson fez, a flowing jellaba and penny-loafers. Help! Here was Haj Ali, the muqaddam, the man in charge of this quarter of the medina. Speaking Arabic, Ramzi salaamed and launched into baroque greetings but for once, Haj Ali cut Ramzi short.

'There's no need for that today. What are doing here? I expected to find you at Riad Waqi—'

'I did an errand.'

'What about the inspector from the Police Judiciaire? He's waiting for me at your riad.'

'That was quick.'

'Quick? My God you're a cool customer. Well don't expect me to be part of your alibi—'

'What?'

'Don't pretend you didn't know. The murder! Hop on.'

Murder? Ramzi swung a leg over the back of the moped. The engine groaned as they darted through a kids' football game and twisted into a tunnelled alleyway. The pedestrians scattered and Haj Ali, with a swivel of the handlebars, outwitted a psychopathic sheep.

Swinging into the cul-de-sac the moped drew up at Riad Waqi. Haj Ali parked and glanced nervously over his shoulder. Ramzi unlocked the front door and ushered the muqaddam in. But turning into the courtyard they ran into Latifa flashing a meat-axe.

Haj Ali leapt back with a scream, nearly knocking Ramzi down. A well-dressed man stood up from a table and introduced himself as Inspector Karim. At the projection of authority Haj Ali calmed down. After a verbal seesaw of greetings, compliments and blessings Ramzi showed the Inspector and the muqaddam to another, larger table.

'La shukran!'—they declined refreshments. Latifa swapped the meat-axe for a broom and now swept the brick floor of the courtyard just within earshot. The inspector traced the geometries of the mosaic table-top with his right index finger and began talking.

That morning they'd found a young man, a European, murdered in Hivernage off the Rue de

Paris. No ID, but they'd received the report from the Tourist Police about Paul Gallisot not returning to the riad, and the description matched.

'Do you happen to know if he left his passport here? I'd like to see his photograph. For identification.'

'Yes, in the safe. I'll just be a minute.'

In the office, Ramzi tapped in the combination. He took out the travel wallet Paul had given him, and unzipped it.

The passport and a couple of credit cards were inside. But what astounded Ramzi was the amount of money—several thousand euros. He had no time to count it. Perplexed, he shut the office door. He re-zipped the wallet and returned it to the safe. On impulse he opened the passport, and on the printer scanned the page with Paul's photo. Strolling back, he placed the passport on the mosaic table.

'Is that the man you found?' Inspector Karim studied the picture and nodded.

'Well, don't blame me,' said Haj Ali. 'Nothing like this has happened before. Thanks to me this quarter of the medina is very law-abiding.' He chuckled. 'No thrill killers around here!'

'That's good news,' Inspector Karim said.

'How did he die?' Ramzi said.

Latifa's broom swished a little closer.

'Somebody cut his throat.'

The broom stopped.

'That was a bit barbaric.'

Inspector Karim looked at Ramzi with interest. 'It was messy. He obviously took the victim by surprise, and Monsieur Gallisot put up quite a struggle to defend himself.'

'How can you tell?'

'The young man's hands were lacerated. The first time the knife entered the throat it rocked in the wound, and the second time the cut was jagged.'

'Did you say "he"? Have you caught the murderer already?'

'No. But the third cut was so violent that it sliced through the neck and severed tissues from the vertebra. It would have required great strength—'

Pale, the muqaddam scraped back his chair and got to his feet. 'Air, I need fresh air—'

As they were already in a courtyard open to the skies, Ramzi knew what was about to happen.

'My rosemary!' Latifa cried out.

Down on his knees by an orange tree, Ramzi checked Haj Ali's head, but saved by the bushes, there was no bleeding. After checking his pulse, he turned him on his side. The fez had slipped off. Ramzi grabbed it and stuffed it under the muqaddam's ankles to elevate his legs.

'Very professional,' Inspector Karim said.

'I used to volunteer with a Mountain Rescue Team in Scotland.'

Haj Ali moaned and tried get up as Latifa replaced a shoe. Ramzi and Inspector Karim steered him to the chair. En route, he stepped on his hat.

'My fez!'

Ramzi picked it up, and Haj Ali took it with dismay. He put a hand inside, trying to straighten out the red felt. Dancing along the table-top, the crumpled fez with its tassel seemed like a glove puppet with swinging black hair.

'Could I have a glass of water please?' it appeared to say.

Ramzi longed to laugh, a reflex to relieve his own shock, but he recalled how he'd offended Dr Rashida earlier. Instead, he flew to the kitchen, paused to compose himself, and returned grim-faced, bearing a tray with a bottle of *Sidi Harazem* and a glass.

'Thank you. I don't know what happened' Haj

Ali said.

'You fainted,' Latifa said. 'And you're the muqaddam!'

His eyes widened. Coughing, he spluttered water. At last, he managed, 'Can we keep it our little secret?'

'Well, there is a matter you could help me with—'

'Name it—'

Meantime, Ramzi turned to the Inspector, suggesting they visit Paul's room.

'Perfect. Lead the way.'

'Up these stairs—'

'Do you recall if Paul Gallisot wore a watch?'

'Yes, he did: a Rolex.'

On the landing Inspector Karim paused. 'The victim carried no valuables, and we suspect that the motive might have been robbery.'

Ramzi decided against disclosing what he'd discovered under the bedcover. Instead he offered up his own theory.

'The first sheep of *Eid al-Adha*?'

'Meaning?'

'Perhaps the murder intended to make a statement.'

'That Paul Gallisot died a humiliating death?'

'Exactly.'

The Brandenburg Concerto Number Three cut in. Inspector Karim pulled a mobile from his jacket and walked off to take the call.

'That was Mme Claval at the French Consulate. Paul Gallisot's sister arrives tomorrow around lunchtime. At some stage, she may want to come here. Or talk to you.'

Ramzi slid back the bolt to Paul Gallisot's room and swung open the door. Inspector Karim stopped Ramzi from stepping inside.

'This might be a secondary crime scene. I'll have to call in forensics.'

'To examine the entire riad? Or just the room? We have guests arriving late afternoon.'

'Just the room. Forensics will be gone by then.'

To speed things along Ramzi pointed to the bed.

'That's strange. It looks like a bump.'

Inspector Karim took a latex glove from his pocket. Pulling it on, he flipped back the bedcover, revealing the wallet, phone and Rolex. He looked at Ramzi between narrowed eyes. This time Ramzi managed not to blush.

EIGHT

'So, I nearly needed a second mortgage to pay the dentist for that root canal.'

'Next time try the old codger who yanked out that teenager's tooth on Djemma el-Fna.'

'Poor boy. The only thing missing was a mini jackhammer on the box beside the dentures. More vino, anyone?'

The guests drank and made merry till the early hours, one of the drawbacks of owning a guesthouse. In the wake of Paul Gallisot's murder Ramzi found the peals of laughter harrowing. Forensics had photographed and fingerprinted Paul's room. But sleep eluded Ramzi because he'd withheld evidence from Inspector Karim. Not the wallet and Rolex, items that undermined the idea Paul was robbed. He'd ultimately cooperated with these. But he didn't let on about the cash in the travel wallet, ten thousand euros in total, and tried to convince himself it corroborated Paul's story about buying carpets. Ramzi had also kept quiet about Paul's trip to see a

Moroccan woman in the Ourika Valley. Just to pile on the guilt, he had secretly copied Paul's passport on the scanner before surrendering it.

How chilling to think that a few hours after their conversation Paul lay in the street, his throat grinning at the stars. Yet he must have realized he was taking a degree of risk as he had left behind his valuables. Still, he couldn't have expected to be murdered. After all, he'd wanted a taxi to the airport. Falling back on scientific method Ramzi tried to formulate various hypotheses, but a motive was hard to fathom. What he needed to do was collect data.

Ramzi wondered exactly where Paul lived in Marrakech last year. He'd mentioned an apartment with a view to the Majorelle Garden, a tourist magnet not far from the medina. He decided to take a walk in that direction the following day, and with that resolution, he finally slept, oblivious, for once, to the summons of fijar prayer.

He awoke before Latifa arrived. Leaving the warmth of the bed, Ramzi opened the shutters and gasped. A human body lay spread-eagled in the courtyard.

Horrified, Ramzi darted down, still wearing a T-shirt and sleep shorts. He recognized David, one of the new guests. Hearing clear sounds of breathing, Ramzi turned him over. An ugly red stain spread across the man's chest. Ramzi's head started spinning, but then he spotted the bottle of Cabernet on the ground nearby. Shaken awake, David sat up, shivered and rubbed his eyes.

Dazed, he complimented Ramzi on the previous night's dinner, a lamb, prune and almond *tajine*, or 'Tangiers' as he put it. Helping him up, Ramzi led him towards the bedroom, but he appeared anxious not to disturb his wife. Ramzi changed tack. Still heavy with sleep, David clung to Ramzi as they staggered towards the *b'hou*, the alcove with a daybed and seats off one side of the courtyard. As he dropped onto the large sofa, he fell on his back, dragging Ramzi down with him.

'Emily—' he said.

The front door slammed and the riad shook. On the sofa Ramzi struggled to untangle himself as a pair of wandering hands rucked up the back of his T-shirt.

'Monsieur Ramzi!'

In a few seconds Latifa stood above them with her broom, rapping Ramzi on the back.

'Emily!'

'Monsieur Ramzi!' He struggled free from the guest's delirious embrace. As Ramzi rearranged himself, David started to snore.

'It's time you found yourself a wife,' Latifa said.

Embarrassed, Ramzi beat a retreat to shower. After dressing, Ramzi settled downstairs in the office. For a few seconds it seemed a sanctuary, then the door hurled open. For the third time in twenty-four hours, Latifa collared him about paying for her mother's medicine, but in all conscience Ramzi couldn't accept the dirhams, even if it dented her pride. Instead he changed the subject.

'You haven't seen a man skulking in the lane? I don't want the guests thinking they risk being mugged every time they come and go.'

'No, I haven't Monsieur Ramzi. But if I do you mustn't worry. No one scares me.'

That he could believe. After dealing with some booking enquiries and a few business matters with Hisham, Ramzi noticed the guests had gone to the roof terrace for breakfast, leaving David still out for the count. Dutifully, he tramped up to greet them. They assured Ramzi they'd enjoyed the previous evening, which he thought just as well given the noise they'd made. Even so, he ground his teeth over the comment that the coffee tasted 'a bit peculiar.' He hoped to hotfoot it when the woman at the head of the table apologized for her husband making such an exhibition of himself earlier that morning.

'It's nothing to worry about,' Ramzi smiled. 'And may I say what a devoted husband you have! He even fell asleep with your name on his lips. Emily, Emily—'

The remark sent a frisson round the breakfast table.

'Actually, my name is Vanessa. This is Emily.'

Vanessa pointed towards the woman beside her, whose hand shook as she lifted her cup to take a sip of coffee. The other two men froze, their bread and jam hovering in mid-air, and the third woman at the table spluttered into her orange juice. Without further hesitation, Ramzi made an excuse and fled.

Grabbing his wallet and keys, he hurried out the front door. In the lane, he could hear recriminations flapping down from the roof terrace. A woman—no, a man—started sobbing and a voice shouted his name. At a gallop, Ramzi made a break for it.

Via a small archway in the ramparts, he left the medina behind. On Avenue du 11 Janvier, he a cut through the Afriquia petrol station and crossed Yacoub Al Mansour, where he dodged a stream of spirited teens with books and bags departing high school. Minutes later Ramzi turned right towards the Majorelle Garden, with a line of taxis and horses and calèches along the wall. But something was odd. No line of tourists. He'd witnessed a miracle.

He recalled Paul said he'd lived behind the garden, so that discounted the brown flats in a compound opposite the entrance, and dictated a trek around the garden's periphery.

In a zig-zag, he sidestepped palm trees exploding out of the tarmac and pink and yellow trumpet vines flopping over walls. Just by the Pharmacie Kenzra and the Café Ponsiette on the corner, the road curved left. The first block of apartments was under construction, so easily eliminated. But the balconies of the second block were positioned in such a way that they faced to the Majorelle Garden, and their view appeared uninterrupted.

Five stories high, the building had steps leading to green wrought iron gates at its entrance. A red Rabat rug had been thrown over one balcony, another had white curtains pulled across it. Opposite, a man lounged in a plastic chair against a pink wall. After a few formalities in Arabic, the man introduced himself as the concierge, Abdul Majid.

Ramzi showed him the scan of the passport. Abdul Majid zipped up his black leather jacket, in what seemed a defensive gesture.

'Yes, that's Monsieur Paul. I remember him. He lived up on the third floor. Now a Lebanese couple live there. But why are you asking me this?'

With that, Abdul Majid looked sulky, and disinclined to go on. Feeling like a second-rate private detective, Ramzi pulled out his wallet to dangle a hundred dirham note. The concierge slipped it into his pocket.

'You remind me of Madame Nicole.'

'Who's Madame Nicole?'

'Monsieur Paul's wife.'

'He's married?'

'Yes.'

'And why do I remind you of his wife?'

'She gave me money, like you just did. I helped her, and she helped me.' He said this with a smile. But the expression had something about it

Ramzi didn't like.

'So, when did the Gallisots leave?'

'That's easy. Last May, after the Casablanca bombings. It was very sudden. First Madame Nicole left. Monsieur Paul packed up and went about a month later. But they'd taken the apartment till October.'

'And when did you see him last?'

'Like I said, last year.'

A car drew up, a woman swung out and asked Abdul Majid for assistance with her shopping. Ramzi decided not to linger, thanked him for the help, and retraced his steps. Paul's marriage caught him off-guard. Paul had given the impression when he talked about Marrakech that he lived here alone. But perhaps the marriage broke up, which would explain his silence, and the abrupt way the couple left Morocco.

Ramzi found himself back at the Café Ponsiette. Taking a table, he ordered a bottle of *Oulmès* sparkling mineral water. On impulse, he showed the waiter the photo.

'That's Monsieur Paul. Sometimes he and Madame Nicole used to come here for breakfast. But then one day they vanished.'

The waiter hadn't seen Paul since, not even in the last few days. He and the concierge Abdul Majid confirmed one thing: Paul hadn't gone back to visit the apartment as he claimed. It reinforced Ramzi's doubts about Paul's real motive for returning to Marrakech.

Ramzi's mobile rang. 'Hisham?'

'Mr David and Mrs Vanessa are leaving!'

'What? Stop them!'

'I can't. They leave on the afternoon flight—'

'How did they book so quickly?'

'They made me do it, Monsieur Ramzi.'

'Have they paid?'

'I pleaded with them—'

'Well, don't pay the taxi.'

'I'll call Kasim.'

'Kasim? Of all people! His driving terrifies the guests—'

'Exactly!'

'Good thinking. Tell him to go the long way.'

Ramzi rang off, paid, left a tip and quit the café. What a fiasco. Deciding it best to lie low for a couple of hours, he bought a ticket to the Majorelle Gardens and sauntered in.

As ever, the audacious blue the original owner

and artist, Jacques Majorelle, had used to paint his art deco studio, its walls and pergolas, exerted a power that inspired visitors to maintain a respectful silence. As Ramzi strolled along the red pathways, he wondered to what extent the Islamic idea of Paradise influenced the painter, as the intoxicating mix of palms, cacti and climbers gave the illusion of growing out of the sky. In the linear pool, the carp flashed between the water lilies.

The path continued under a vault of black-stemmed bamboo where a flock of tourists ambled in his direction. Stepping aside, he turned away and read some of the graffiti carved into the thick bamboo trunks. FRED+LULU POUR TOUJOURS. SHIT HOT. ANTONIO+ZINEB. KARIM MOHAMED. EDUARDO ANA. The usual stuff, but the delight was: FAIRY+DOUGHNUT.

The tourists trailed by. But as Ramzi started towards the exit another name caught his eye. Nicole. He doubled back. PAUL+NICOLE+TAHAR.

Tahar. T, pronounced *Ta*, and h, pronounced *Ha*, were the opening letters of the twentieth *sura* in the Qur'an, and a name synonymous with Muhammed.

It seemed too much of a coincidence for Paul

and Nicole to be anybody other than Paul and Nicole Gallisot. But who was Tahar?

As Ramzi considered this, a sense of unreality came over him. His heart started pounding, so much so he settled on a bench for a few minutes to recover.

When he stood up to leave, he felt as though he had started on the road to a discovery as vital as any in his scientific career. And for the first time in months he noticed a slight spring in his step.

NINE

'You must buy a sheep, Monsieur Ramzi, before they run out,' Latifa said.

Ramzi reminded her sheep were everywhere, plus he didn't think their guests would appreciate the courtyard being turned into an abattoir. Latifa suggested they hide it in the laundry and do the deed whilst the guests went off sightseeing. Ramzi recalled they had lamb in the freezer, at which she threw up her hands in horror, and retreated to the kitchen, exasperated.

Paul Gallisot's sister had asked to see him at around ten. The appointment was convenient, as it meant he'd avoid any goodbyes with the two remaining couples from David and Vanessa's coterie. So, an hour before, he set off towards Bab Doukkala. Rounding a corner, he leapt like a ballerina to cheat being crippled by the wheels of a cannonballing handcart; inside it a dark-faced ram rattled to its doom. What had Latifa said? Sheep were in short supply? *Per contra.* In the modern city, sheep were everywhere, lining up at bus stops, lingering at cafés, leering at shop windows, lurking at ATMs and taking in the sights.

The day was mellow and the trees lining Mohammed V surrendered the scent of orange blossom. At the avenue's vanishing point the minaret of the Koutoubia Mosque stood like a glowing sentinel. Rainbows flashed in the spray of the fountain at the Place de la Liberté. Here Ramzi crossed to Hivernage, Marrakech's zone of hotels, villas and gardens. The labyrinth of the medina quickly embedded into the subconscious, but Ramzi remained disoriented by colonial France's passion for interlinking stars of avenues and roads. At last, tired of the trim streets that seemed to go on forever, he found the Rue de Paris. Off it, he spotted a rookie standing guard beside a cordon of yellow tape, emblazoned in English with CRIME SCENE DO NOT CROSS, more Miami than Marrakech.

Alongside, dry bracts of bougainvillea spilled over a high wall. But the rust-red stains on the ground were not pigment from the leaves. Ramzi's heart clenched. Until this minute Paul Gallisot's murder appeared academic. Now it brought home the naked fact that a human being, someone he knew, had died here in brutal circumstances.

Quickening his pace, he reached the Hotel Es-Saadi. Concrete blocks barricaded the drive, a precaution Ramzi suspected was taken after the Casablanca bombings last May. In the lobby, he recognized Madame Claval, a lady he'd met at various *vernissages* and cocktail parties. Crossing to the sofa, Ramzi greeted her and she introduced Héloïse Bertonnet, Paul Gallisot's sister, dressed in *haute couture* black.

A waiter arrived and asked if he wanted anything. Before Ramzi could reply, Héloïse snapped back, 'Stop bothering us,' and waved the man away.

Shocked, Ramzi apologized to the waiter in Arabic and to keep clear-witted ordered a double expresso.

'Well, do you know if the police have caught my brother's killer? No one seems to be able to give me a straight answer, but that's just typical of a country like Morocco. I really can't imagine why anyone would want to murder Paul. Can you? You do understand what I am saying, don't you?'

At this opening volley, Madame Claval shot Ramzi a look. Paul's sister had used the formal *vous* of

French with her, yet addressed Ramzi in the familiar *tu*. He imagined that true to her family's colonial background, she used *tu* as the French had in Algeria, a derogatory term reserved for intimates, domestics, animals—and Arabs.

'Monsieur Ramzi has a doctorate in physics from Oxford University,' Madame Claval said. 'He—'

'I barely knew him,' Ramzi said, interrupting her.

'What sort of answer is that?'

'He seemed pleasant enough. But I have no idea if the probability of your brother being murdered was high or low.'

Madame Clavel jumped to her feet, promised to return with paperwork to sign, and almost collided with the waiter bearing the double expresso. Alone, Héloïse and Ramzi sat in silence for a few moments.

'Paul did tell me you lived in Algeria as children.'

'My mother had been raised in French Algeria. Her family once owned a citrus farm called Mafleury on the Mitidja Plain before abandoning it at independence. My father was a petrochemical engineer. After they were married she encouraged him to work in Algeria, even after it nationalized

French oil. But we were barely teenagers when the country began to collapse into civil war. One of our father's colleagues was found with his throat cut—'

Héloïse stopped mid-sentence, realizing what she'd said, and raised diamond clad fingers across her neck.

'They called it the Kabylie smile.'

Ramzi drained the expresso, grimacing at the smack of chicory. Héloïse interpreted this as a sympathetic gesture, and relaxed a little. After a moment, she continued with the family story.

'We returned to France, to Nice. After leaving the *lycée*, Paul went to university to study engineering. That's how he met Nicole one Easter, on the crossing to Algiers. He planned to visit to Mafleury to check out what happened to the estate since independence. Well he found out all right. He found those—those *ratons* burned it to the ground after my mother's family left.'

Ratons: young rats? Ignoring this second racist slur, Ramzi asked about Nicole.

Héloïse pursed her lips. 'Let's say, I never warmed to her.'

He wondered if Héloïse liked anybody much, but she went on.

'She was dragged up in one of those dodgy suburbs, Clichy-sous-Bois I think, to the east of Paris. I don't even know how she got into university. Maybe because she chose to read Arabic—'

'Arabic?'

'Quite! In any event, they probably only let her in because of her background, a sort of social experiment. And just as Nicole wormed her way into university, she wormed her way into Paul's life.

'They married after they graduated. I thought from the first she was a fortune hunter.' Héloïse laughed, revealing gold fillings. 'But now with Paul's death she can't get one euro of the family's money. I suppose there's a small consolation in that. Things rather backfired on her.'

'In what way?'

'Nicole pushed Paul into taking the job in Marrakech. Why leave a career at a prestigious engineering company in Paris?'

'It sounds like history repeating itself.' 'And what do you mean by that?'

'What you said about your mother encouraging your father to work in Algeria—'

'This was different. They barely stayed in Morocco a year. Nicole left last May. Paul said Nicole had been unwell. I imagined he meant they'd separated, and how right I was. In no time Nicole had her old job back in Paris, at the Arab World Institute. But with Paul it was different.'

'Why?'

'He seemed changed. Unfocussed. Can you imagine it? He rented a room and started working in a bookshop!'

'Does Nicole know about your brother's death?'

'The consulate contacted her and she called me from Paris. By the tone of her voice anyone might imagine Paul had simply caught a cold.'

'Where is she now?'

'She's coming later today for the funeral tomorrow.'

'It's in Marrakech?'

'The consulate suggested Paul be buried at the European cemetery. It seems sensible. My mother died a couple of years ago. That, coupled with the worry over Paul, put my father under a lot of pressure. He had a heart attack and needed a triple by-pass after Christmas. He's too weak to travel at the moment, but if we buried Paul in France, I think the stress might be fatal.'

'Are you having a service?'

'Ten o'clock. At the *Église des Saints Martyrs*. Naturally, the coffin will be closed. The church should be packed. After all there's myself, Nicole and Madame Claval. Unless you'd like to help make up the numbers?'

'Of course,' Ramzi said. 'By the way, did you know a friend of your brother's, called Tahar?'

'No,' she said, shaking her head. 'But obviously he never changed.'

'What do you mean?'

'I mean he always had an Arab in tow. Ever since Algeria and Salem.'

'Salem?'

'Our housekeeper's son in Algeria. He and Paul were always disappearing off together. Then at the *lycée* in France the guys Paul hung out with were almost all North Africans.'

'So, you don't know who Tahar is?'

'No. But maybe Nicole does. Why not ask the grieving widow tomorrow?'

TEN

It was a relief to leave Héloïse and the Es-Saadi. Ramzi strolled along a road lined with olive trees towards Avenue Mohammed VI to his branch of BMCE bank to get copies of the missing bank statements he need to keep the accountant, Abdelfattah, sweet. Also, he planned to visit a nearby shop Promart, which sold professional catering equipment, so that he could replace items of broken crockery at Riad Waqi.

So, few people would be at the funeral tomorrow. Ramzi had little appetite for either the wake or the service. He had the bright idea of finding Ingémaroc, Paul Gallisot's old work place, and broadcasting the event to bring in more mourners. But he tried to analyze his motives. Did he feel sorry for Héloïse? Or had he taken running a riad to extremes, rustling up rent-a-crowd for a guest's burial? *It's all part of the service, sir.* Even better, he imagined a paragraph on the website: 'Should you expire during your stay, our management will ensure all measures are taken to guarantee a well-attended funeral.' It could be a unique selling point in a competitive market.

Bank statements in hand, he made his way to Promart. Down in the basement he loaded a basket with a white milk jug, half-a-dozen side plates with a blue and white mosaic pattern, and extra knives and teaspoons. Returning to the checkout the cashier rang up the goods. As Ramzi gave her the tax details of Riad Waqi for the receipt, it struck him that Ingémaroc's address might be on their records. Obligingly she checked the computer, and up it popped.

Just in time, as at one o'clock Promart closed. But the hour also marked the shift changeover for the petit taxis. Finding a ride would be impossible. Also, he suspected Ingémaroc would be closed for lunch. He decided to grab a bite to eat, and settled into a teak chair on one of the boulevard cafés. Beyond the avenue, the Atlas flexed its muscular rock and snow peaks. Rushing between the tourists and designer dressed Moroccans the waiter barely paused to take Ramzi's order of a club sandwich and Schweppes tonic water.

Lunch finished, Ramzi sat jingling the ice in

the glass. Across the avenue, someone hailed a petit taxi: the changeover had ended. The waiter had vanished so Ramzi went inside to the bar to pay. A chandelier dominated the room. *Staying Alive* by the Bee Gees pumped from a stereo. In parallel, a TV screen on the far wall showed the latest carnage in Iraq.

The bill snapped Ramzi back to the present; double what he might have paid elsewhere. A hundred dirhams poorer, he caught a taxi to Ingémaroc. The company turned out to be based in a terraced house close to the Majorelle Garden. The villa's architecture mixed Islamic and Renaissance motifs. Beside the gate a brass plaque read INGÉMAROC SARL. He rang the bell, the gate buzzed open and he climbed a flight of steps to the entrance on the first floor.

The door stood ajar. The reception reeked of cheap perfume. At a desk facing a wall, a young woman arranged her hijab. Ramzi walked up behind her.

'Good afternoon.'

'Hold on a minute.'

In front of her lay a page printed from a website on hijab styles. She flipped it over.

71

'Is this Ingémaroc?'

'It is. Can I help you?'

'Did a man named Paul Gallisot used to work here?'

'Not you as well! I had Inspector Karim from the police here yesterday. People don't appreciate how busy I am.'

'Forgive me for saying this, but I like the way you're wearing your hijab. It's very original.'

'Do you think so?'

'Yes, it suits you.'

'I thought it did. It's the latest fashion.'

'I know you're rushed off your feet, but what was he like?'

'Cute for a cop. Dreamy eyes.'

'Not the inspector, I mean Paul Gallisot.'

'He was pleasant. He always complimented me on how I looked.'

'But?'

'Sometimes he sounded a bit patronizing.'

'And?'

'It's like I told Inspector Karim. I always felt something didn't ring true about Monsieur Paul. Still, I didn't sleep a wink last night over what happened to him. And my boss is a nervous wreck.'

'Oh?'

'It's the second time in nine months the police have investigated our employees.'

'The second time?'

'Yes. The first time was Monsieur Tahar.'

'Tahar?'

'Tahar Sediki. He was a friend of Monsieur Paul. The police interviewed all of us, and came back a couple of times.'

Tahar Sediki. Ramzi smiled. He had a surname.

'Why were the police so interested in him?'

'Remember the suicide bombings in Casablanca last May? That's the weekend Monsieur Tahar disappeared. He took the Friday off and never returned. My boss tried to contact him, but couldn't, and reported him missing to the police.'

'Why, was he a religious extremist?'

'He just seemed a normal guy. Liberal, clean-shaven, western in the way he dressed and acted. But maybe that was a cover, that's what I told the police. You see, I'd seen him with a woman a couple of times.'

'I don't understand. Is that a crime?'

'The woman: she wore a burqa.'

'The full body cloak?'

'Head to toe. Gloves, the lot.'

'That's unusual in Morocco.'

'Well there's Islam, and Islam, as far as I am concerned. It just seemed an odd match.'

'Was he married?'

'No.'

'Or did he have a sister?'

'No, he was an only child. He once told me that.'

'What was he like?'

'He lit up a room, that's what I always thought. But who are you anyway? I'm not sure I should have told you all these things. I think you'd better leave. I've a pile of work to do.'

'One more thing, do you know this name: Zahra Ait El Amri?'

'Never heard of her. But speak to Monsieur Bob. Bob Spasoff. He's American. He and Tahar worked together a lot. Now I really must get on.'

'I almost forgot. I'm here on behalf of the Gallisot family. Is anyone from Ingémaroc planning to go to the funeral?'

'My boss is in Rabat on business for a couple of days. The two new guys didn't know him.'

'And what about the American, Bob Spasoff?'

'He's on a project, south in Zagora.'

'Can you go?'

'The thing is,' she said, 'if I did go, and went alone, people might get the wrong idea about Monsieur Paul and me. I'm sure you understand.'

Ramzi left her to experiment with the latest hijab styles. Swinging the bag of crockery and cutlery, he headed home. The day had brought more questions than answers. First the matter of Paul's search for Zahra Ait El Amri the day before he died. Héloïse intimated there'd been problems between Paul and his wife. So perhaps, as Ramzi originally thought, he had an affair with Zahra: marriage over. Either he confessed or was caught with his pants down. It explained Nicole's sudden departure from Marrakech.

Yet Paul left soon afterwards. Perhaps his new relationship had fizzled out, as often happens, or pressure from a traditional rural family made them split up due to cultural differences. Perhaps Zahra returned to her village and Paul hoped for reconciliation, but thought the better of it. But was Paul's visit to the Ourika Valley associated with his death? Another riddle was Paul's destination the night he died, as he'd taken the precaution of leaving his watch and wallet behind.

Tahar's disappearance at the time of Casablanca bombings seemed equally strange. Perhaps the receptionist was right, his liberal attitudes and appearance were a cover, as betrayed by the woman in the distinctive burqa.

Alternatively, she was of no importance. The attacks occurred at the time Nicole left Marrakech, so it made sense to speculate Nicole and Tahar left together, maybe as lovers. If true, Paul must have known, so why hadn't he told the police? After all, the police returned to Ingémaroc for questioning a couple of times. Maybe shame or embarrassment kept him quiet?

Feeling drained, Ramzi arrived at the avenue. A kid motorcyclist roared past, the bike pulling an old woman strapped in a wheelchair. And above the noise of the traffic, from a nearby minaret, came the call to afternoon prayer.

ELEVEN

'The sky has a blockage of urine.' Such was the saying, as in Morocco the clouded sky is compared to a living being.

'You're right Latifa: there's a storm brewing,' Ramzi said.

'I can't believe it.'

'But you just said—'

'No, forget the sky. You—'

'Me?'

'Dressed like that you look almost European.'

Ramzi wore a dark suit, tailor-made at Davies & Son, Saville Row. His silk twill tie, adorned with flying elephants and ducks, was whimsical, but he hoped at the funeral it was not thought flippant.

Thus, he set off. Outside the riad a woman in a veil sat against a wall, asking for alms, and he dropped a couple of dirhams into her palm. A young woman washed clothes in a bucket at the public fountain. Ramzi stepped aside to avoid the sloshing water, only to be splashed by white-bearded peddler sprinkling mountains of mint further up the lane.

'Hey, watch out!'

'No harm meant monsieur!'

Beyond the medina walls he had better luck. An empty *petit* taxi screeched to a halt, and Ramzi jumped in.

'*L'Église des Saints Martyrs.*'

'*Inshallah.*'

One of the first monuments built by the French in Marrakech, the pink church with the bell tower appeared plucked from Andalusia. It reminded Ramzi of the verse from the Bible, 'your sons and your daughters shall prophesy, and your young men shall see visions, and your old men shall dream dreams.' A policeman stood on guard outside, and he questioned Ramzi at the door, but let him pass. He walked in but, not wanting to disturb the liturgy, took a seat at the back.

After the ceremony ended, pallbearers hoisted the coffin, lumbering up the aisle, three women behind. Ramzi recognized Mme Claval and Héloïse, and the third he guessed must be Paul Gallisot's wife, Nicole. A sharp black trouser suit enhanced a boyish figure and mane of honey blonde hair, whilst over her shoulders she'd thrown, with measured carelessness, a flamboyant scarf.

Ramzi let the coffin and the mourners pass. Outside the church, thunder rumbled in the distance.

'Monsieur Ramzi, may I introduce you to Nicole Gallisot?'

Ramzi offered his condolences as a black limousine drew up.

'The car's here if you're ready to go to the cemetery,' Madame Claval said.

'Monsieur Ramzi.' He turned, and found himself shaking hands with Inspector Karim. They exchanged a few pleasantries, and meantime the hearse pulled out and crawled away, followed by Madame Claval, Héloïse and Nicole in the black limousine. Inspector Karim offered a lift to the cemetery, which Ramzi accepted. Inspector Karim made a call, and they headed around the corner to the HQ of the *Police Judiciare*, where an unmarked car with a driver waited. Setting off, the Inspector was the first to speak.

'As forensics have finished I informed Madame Gallisot she's free to collect her husband's personal effects if she wishes.'

'Did they find anything interesting?'

'Only that your fingerprints seemed to outnumber the housekeeper's.'

Ramzi reddened, shifting in his seat. 'But are you any closer to identifying a suspect?'

'We do have one or two leads. But all I can say at present is that I fear the outcome will be sad for all concerned.'

With those ominous words the car turned into the Rue Erraouda and pulled up outside the European Cemetery. The young driver popped the trunk and leapt out to open the doors. From the rear he pulled out two small bouquets of roses in cellophane.

Inspector Karim gave one to Ramzi, who felt mildly embarrassed for not having been so thoughtful. The hearse crawled through the gates. The three women had left the limo, walking behind.

From the main gate a short avenue led to a white obelisk, a war memorial with the dedication, *Aux combatants Français et Marocain qui ont donnés leurs vies pour la liberté.* Against it lay a wreath tied with a French tricolour ribbon. To the right stretched a field of white crosses, three hundred and thirty-three Foreign Legion soldiers who died during their service to the protectorate. As they inched along behind the cortège Inspector Karim stopped.

He pointed out the graves, side by side. They belonged to two brigadier police, Roland Coulon, aged forty-one and René Mignot, aged thirty, killed on duty on 15 August 1953 during demonstrations in Marrakech against the French occupation. A crucifix of red porcelain roses decorated the headstone of Roland Coulon; the passage of years had cracked the tintype photo of René Mignon. Inspector Karim asked for the bouquet Ramzi held, and placed one on each grave. Ramzi expressed surprise.

'The politics is irrelevant. They were both policemen, killed in the line of duty, and should be remembered as such.'

They caught up with the cortège. Burial rites over, shovel-by-shovel the red earth of Marrakech thudded onto Paul's coffin. A wire of blue lighting seared the sky. After a few moments they turned, and retraced their steps along the Avenue, under a volley of thunder.

By the graves of the two unfortunate policemen, Héloïse stopped.

'Look at those flowers. How wonderful their relatives still remember their sacrifice in the line of duty.'

'How do you know it was their relatives, and not some thoughtful Moroccan or a well-wisher?' Ramzi said.

She pointed to the inscription on the stone.

'Believe it or not I can read. And believe me, no Moroccan would lay flowers in the memory of these two souls.'

Inspector Karim studied his nails, but said nothing.

'Who's going to put flowers on Paul's grave?' Nicole asked.

'I will, of course.'

'Well as you haven't been near your ancestors' mausoleum in Blida, I have my doubts. It's terrible the way your family left Algeria and abandoned them to that awful silence.'

'Isn't that what happens when you're dead?' Héloïse said. 'An awful silence?'

'You misunderstood. You should never abandon someone you love.'

'And what, Nicole, did you ever know about love?'

The air trembled with electricity. Inspector Karim, Madame Claval and Ramzi instinctively stepped aside. But Nicole regained her composure, and walked away.

'I want to go back to the hotel.'

'Of course,' Madame Claval said. 'But what about your sister-in-law?'

'She is the least of my worries.'

'I can take Madame Gallisot back,' Ramzi said.

After exchanging goodbyes, he soon drew level with Nicole. She stood, staring at a mausoleum inspired by the Acropolis. Ramzi adjusted his cuffs, poised to ad lib some platitude, but Nicole spoke first.

'Thank you for rescuing me. This has all been a shock. And this European cemetery, here in North Africa, just makes the pain sharper.'

'I can see you're upset. Paul told me a bit about Algeria.'

'Did he tell you we went to the European cemetery in Blida together? Or he wanted to be buried there? I couldn't bear it if he had. It would have been almost prophetic.'

'No, he didn't.'

Nicole stared dreamily ahead. 'His family's tomb is pretty crass. It's a mock Egyptian pylon. Hieroglyphics everywhere. His great grandfather fancied himself as an Egyptologist. Even though Paul had the key, we had to throw ourselves against the door to open it. Inside were two coffins, and the other shelves empty. But this was the thing. A broom and a zinc pail were tidied into a corner.'

'Well at least the grave-robbers hadn't been.'

Nicole gave a small smile. 'I made much the same comment at the time. But it began to obsess me, the thought of someone, maybe Paul's grandmother, cleaning it for a final time. Then decades of that awful silence.'

She reflected for a second. 'In Algeria Paul said he'd like to be buried in sight of the Atlas. Well at least he got his wish.'

At that, they walked on. Eerily, the sky had taken on a greenish tinge. Amongst the tombstones, a small rattan canopy was rigged between palms, sheltering a few cushions and a small stove with a brass kettle. A little beyond stood rows of simple crosses and one or two angels, marking a children's graveyard.

Nicole put a hand to her mouth, and let out a sob. Poignant though this section of the cemetery might be, the reaction was surprising. So many colonists died young. Marrakech was a city of extremes, and people either died early or lived to ripe old age.

'Yes, children—' he began.

'Paul and I: we never had a child.'

From all he'd heard, that appeared plain, and Ramzi had touched a nerve.

Nicole looked up. 'It's almost overhead. Isn't thunder supposed to be the noise made by a voiceless angel trying to talk and pray to God? Now the lightening. He's moved his wings.'

Before he could remark, she stepped in front of him and, to his astonishment, straightened his tie.

'My twin.'

Ramzi jumped, at first unsure what she meant. Speaking French, she used the phrase, *mon semblable.*

'—*Hypocrite lecteur, —mon semblable, —mon frère.*' Ramzi quoted in reply.

'Ah, Baudelaire. Are you accusing me, like he accused his readers, of being as guilty of sins and lies as the poet?'

'No, it just flew into my head. But what did you mean?'

'Your tie: my scarf. Both *Hermès.*'

If sky was heavy, so was their silence as they walked to the cemetery gate.

'I want you to show me Paul's room.'

'At the riad? *D'accord*.'

Ramzi stepped into the road to hail a taxi. A sheep sporting a cowboy hat peered out of the rear window of a passing van.

Nicole laughed, but caught herself. 'How awful, laughing at Paul's funeral. You must think I'm terrible.'

Raindrops splashed against Ramzi's face. In the nick of time a *petit* taxi drew up. They climbed in, just before a deluge defeated the swipes of the windscreen wipers. Hailstones hammered the roof, and ricocheted off the road.

The taxi edged onto Avenue du 11 Janvier. Through the hail the medina walls appeared to dissolve and vanish. Cars and buses ploughed through rivers of water. With a rag, the driver wiped the windscreen, but it still steamed up. Rolling down his window, he asked them to do the same. Turning towards the gateway of Bab Yacout a cacophony of car horns besieged them. Ahead, a donkey cart laden with sacks of concrete and reinforcing rods caused a jam. Ramzi winced as the owner took a stick to the stubborn beast. The donkey stretched its neck and began to bray. The cart jolted and inched forward.

The taxi crawled alongside, but as it drew parallel the donkey brayed again, and its muzzle came through the open window, showing its lips, teeth and tongue. Nicole yelped and pulled away.

'Are we nearly there?' She sounded like a child.

'It's just around that corner.'

To his amazement, Nicole scrambled over him, threw open the door and half falling into the street, disappeared into the downpour, along the only road. Handing over fifty dirhams that far exceeded the fare, Ramzi told the driver to keep the change. Turning up his jacket collar, he slid out, slammed the door and dashed off in pursuit, suit soaked and hail stinging his face and hands. To think he'd been bothered by the herb-seller's spatter of water!

TWELVE

'I am the emissary of bad news' Hisham said.

'Can we talk later?' Ramzi said.

He and Nicole had reached Riad Waqi as the hail eased into rain. Pouring off the pantiles, water plummeted down every side of the courtyard, creating cascades that dwarfed the luminous trees. Latifa swept the ice towards the drain, but Ramzi, worried she'd get drenched and he'd never hear the end of it, dispatched her to make mint tea. Picking their way across the crushed ice, he showed Nicole to the salon. Almost at once she read aloud the Arabic panel above the hearth, *The weight of the burden is known only by he who carries it.* And like her husband before, she looked preoccupied for a brief moment.

Mystified, Ramzi knelt down to light the fire. The hairs rose on the back of his neck, and he hoped it wasn't a bad omen. She slipped off her scarf. Beneath it hung a silver amulet. He recognized it as a Taureg piece.

'Have you got something inside it?'

'Yes, yes I do.' And it was clear she wasn't going to volunteer more. Ramzi excused himself, and ran upstairs to change his jacket for a jumper, and to find a fresh towel for Nicole.

Back in the salon she'd taken down a book on Orientalist artists, browsing through the paintings that included work by Delacroix, Regnault, Gerôme, Baratti. Grateful for the towel, she dried her hair in small bunches, leaving a faint scent of chamomile in the room. Latifa's appearance with a brass tray bearing a silver teapot brought Ramzi back to earth.

'May I introduce you to Madame Gallisot—'

Latifa scowled and the tray clattered onto the table with such force that one of the tea glasses fell over, and the little Moroccan cakes jumped on their plate.

'Thank you, Latifa.'

Latifa narrowed her eyes, and left, muttering. Ramzi arranged the tray on the table. Nicole preferred just a hint of sugar. He poured tea into a glass, returned it to the pot, and poured it out again, raising the spout to a dramatic height.

Commenting on the book, Ramzi admired the beauty of some of the paintings, especially the portraits of Islamic architecture.

'Really? Look at how the men are portrayed: predatory, usually dark-skinned or black, usually ugly and loathsome, and usually with brutal and shifty, unsympathetic expressions.'

Nicole flipped pages back and forth, drawing attention to the recurring images of daggers, swords, and pistols, and bracelets, rings and jewels.

'Here we have the mythical East: explosive and dangerous, totally unfit to control its wealth. A perfect pretext for colonialism.'

'It's the same now,' Ramzi said. 'Except photographers have replaced the artists. All we see are photos of car bombs, body parts and wrecked homes and frightening shots of angry or grief-stricken people. Of course, now the weapons are nuclear and chemical, and the riches are oil and gas.'

'We think alike.'

'Please, help yourself to a *corne de gazelle*.'

Nicole took a bite of the pastry and marzipan.

'Where do your blue eyes come from?' she said.

'From my Scottish father and my Moroccan mother. Not everyone in North Africa has brown eyes.'

'Yes, I—' Nicole began, but left the sentence unfinished. Instead she said, 'My best friend Hassiba is a *beur*,' she said.

'I almost wish there was an equivalent slang term in Britain for the younger generation born there, but lost between two cultures, two languages, two histories. I always felt the term *beur* gave a positive sense of identity to France's North African immigrants, a sense of being included. Since I was a kid, I've been called a Paki, which is not only offensive but also inaccurate. But let's get back to you. Héloïse told me you grew up in Clichy-sous-Bois. What was it like?'

'Let me see. I lived in a sixteenth floor flat in a tower block; the elevators never worked; the stairs smelt of piss; graffiti decorated the walls; at street level metal grills clad shop fronts, doors and windows. No metro ran there, and the nearest commissariat was in Raincy. Sometimes I can still smell the concrete. And when I do, it lingers at the back of my throat.

'Most of my friends were *beurs* like Hassiba. They hung out together, and though they all spoke French, I picked up bits of Arabic, collecting words and phrases like my friends collected music or makeup. My parents knew I mixed with the *beurs* but it was still a case of out of sight, out of mind, until one day when I was fourteen Hassiba gave me a caftan. That evening I hennaed my hair, whitened my teeth and reddened my gums with a piece of sweet-chestnut bark. I went to show my parents. They were watching TV. My father flipped out. I tried to run, but he barred the door. And then, well look, I've still this scar.'

The sight of it, small though it was, dismayed Ramzi. But to his surprise Nicole excused her father. He'd married late. He'd done military service during the Algerian War, and afterwards drifted. Sometimes when he'd drunk too much—a common occurrence—he'd tell her things about what he did in the army, such as making the Algerians they captured talk.

'He said it was very tiring.'

'Tiring?' Ramzi said.

'Sometimes they worked a ten-hour day in the cellar. The problem was when to let the next guy have a go. My father used to say, "Just as the bird softened up we didn't want the next chap to have the privilege or glory of it. You had to have the flair for it to know when to lay off and when to lay on. You see, hope is what made them tell the truth.'"

Ramzi found this chilling, and said so.

'Really? It makes me sad.'

'About your father?'

'The world imposed on him. He tortured Arabs for his country, "for the greater good" as he often put it, and for a lost cause. Afterwards he saw Algerians welcomed in France as the country needed cheap labour. They lived on our doorstep, ensuring that the past tormented him. And in the unkindest cut of all, the culture and language he had been forced to hate cast a spell and stole me away.'

'And you married the son of a French colonial *pied noir*—'

'Ironic, isn't it? What a family! They still live in the past apparently unaware of De Gaulle's words, "Papa's Algeria is dead." Instead they sit and watch old cine films of their citrus farm Mafleury. It's pitiful really. They weep with nostalgia as the camera pans across the citrus groves. Then the movie climaxes with the Dumont picnic on Easter Monday. Imagine, the family in floral frocks and hats and lightweight suits, waited on by two Algerian servants wearing white gloves. Toasting the camera with champagne, and on to the ceremonial breaking of the *mouna*—'

'The *mouna*?'

'A cake soaked with orange flower water. The whole scene made me want to put the celluloid into acid. It was even stranger for me. I had been there with Paul, just after we met. There'd been a fire that reduced the house and the outbuildings to a shell. The only thing we discovered intact was an icehouse. His grandfather used to collect cartloads of snow from the Atlas in the winter and pack it for the summer to make sorbets. Decades ago: pre-fridges and freezers. Anyhow, Paul flew into a tirade against the Algerians for torching the family home. Another irony.'

'In what way?'

'It wasn't the Algerians: the pyromaniacs were Paul's mother Catherine and his grandfather. And do you know how they justified their actions? By blaming the Arab mentality. Algeria may have won independence, but the Arabs had to understand the significance of what was happening. If the French couldn't remain, they would return Algeria to what it was when they invaded in 1830. "We created it, so we can destroy it," that's what they thought. So, they doused the buildings on the estate with petrol, and whoosh, up it all went. In the end it was no surprise, at least to me, that his mother killed herself.'

'She committed suicide?'

'The official report concluded she drowned. But believe me, Catherine could out-swim Djullanar the Sea-girl. I know it sounds crazy, but I think she was swimming towards Algeria. Sometimes she imagined she could see North Africa across the Mediterranean, from their house near Nice. She ached to go back.'

Nicole fingered the Tuareg amulet around her neck. Ramzi refilled the tea glasses.

'Paul didn't seem to be anything like his mother. He seemed to me pleasant and outgoing.' Nicole sipped the tea, and reflected that although genial, Paul had a temper.

'That's one reason we came to Marrakech, because of something that happened with his father.'

'Were they close?'

'Not exactly. After Paul graduated, he planned to travel and do voluntary work overseas, maybe in Indochina, or Sub-Saharan Africa. He asked his father for a loan, but his father put his foot down, saying it would wreck any hope of a career. He suggested various options in Southern France, but Paul defiantly told him he'd apply to companies in Paris. Almost immediately he landed a job on the payroll of an engineering consultancy, off the Boulevard Haussmann. We got caught up in the popping of champagne corks, Paul proposed and we married a few weeks later. In Paris, our lives seemed golden. Everything remained hunky-dory until Paul bumped into the CEO in the lift. He asked Paul how his father was. It took Paul by surprise. He replied he hadn't realized he knew him. It turned out Paul's father put some work their way a few years ago, and asked him to keep a look out for Paul's c.v. Payback time, I expect.

'Paul came home and went into tailspin. He kept saying, "I'm tired of living a lie." Next day he started job hunting and lo and behold he spotted an ad for an engineer with a company in Marrakech.

'It put me in a fix. Marriage was important, but so was my work.'

The quandary made Ramzi's heart quicken. 'Yet in the end you came?'

'As a compromise, I begged a leave of absence. But the week we planned to leave Paris for Marrakech, I had a call from my mother. My father's skin had turned yellow and tests diagnosed liver cancer.'

'Playing the dutiful daughter gave me a good

excuse to delay joining Paul. I ran around like a ministering angel. A couple of months later my father's body began to shut down, and he became delusional. He kept seeing people who weren't there, people from the Algerian war. The things he said, I'll never forget them.

'I held his hand. "Papa, it was wrong." And he kept saying, "But I was good at it. I was good at it." I felt such relief when I heard the breathing stop. But there was no repentance, even when the priest came to give the last rites. No confession, no contrition. Repentance: I think that has been left to me.'

For a few moments, they sat until Nicole broke the silence.

'But I'll confess something. I cried. Not for my father, but because I knew I'd have to go to Morocco.'

'I'll confess something too. Paul said you lived in an apartment near the Majorelle Garden. Out of curiosity I went to see where he lived. That's how I found out about you. From the concierge, remember Abdul Majid?'

'Abdul Majid? He's never there when you want him and always there when you don't!'

Startled, Ramzi switched the subject. 'Do you

know someone called Tahar Sediki?' Nicole drained her tea and replaced the glass. 'Why do you ask?' 'On the way back from your apartment, I went for a stroll round the Majorelle Garden. I was standing on the pathway lined with bamboo and carved on one of the canes I saw three names: Nicole, Paul and Tahar.'

After a moment of hesitation, Nicole said, 'Was that my phone?'

She fumbled in her shoulder bag and checked a mobile. 'I must have been mistaken. Where were we?'

'Bamboo. Names.'

'I recall now. Tahar was a colleague of Paul's. Paul carved our names on the bamboo for fun. In fact, I'm surprised they're still there.'

'Did you know Tahar disappeared?'

The question hung in the air.

'Yes,' Nicole said.

Unsure how to go on, Ramzi suggested they see Paul's room and she agreed.

Outside the only sign of the rain and hail were the trees dripping and a few fallen oranges. He led Nicole up to the bedroom off the gallery. The room had been left more or less as it was, except the small bump under the duvet had gone. She wandered around, making her way to the bathroom. At the washbasin, she fingered Paul's toothbrush and toiletries. Then she stiffened, pointing to the bottle of *Eau Sauvage* cologne.

'This was Paul's?'

Ramzi nodded. Picking up the bottle, she unscrewed the silver cap and sprayed a little on her wrist. The scent, fresh and virile, dominated the bathroom. Nicole sat on the deep sill of the window.

Then, for no reason he could discern, the blood drained from Nicole's face and for a few moments she resembled a waxwork from a museum. He called her name, but received no response. About to check for a pulse, she rallied. For a moment she looked disorientated, tears welled up in her eyes and rolled down her cheeks. Ramzi's first reaction was to put an arm round her shoulder, but he thought it inappropriate in the circumstances. Embarrassed, he slinked away to waited outside the bedroom, until she joined him.

'I'm sorry about that—'

'I've put your husband's wallet and the Rolex in the safe. The police took his phone and passport.'

'I'll give the watch to Héloïse for her son. He

always admired it.'

'Héloïse seemed to think that you and Paul had split up.'

'That's none of your business. But I suppose it doesn't really matter. Yes, we had. But we never discussed divorce.'

'There's the matter of the travel wallet. Paul left quite a lot of money inside.'

'Oh?'

'About ten thousand euros.'

'Why on earth—?'

'He said he was buying rugs, but apparently he didn't find any.'

A silence ensued, but a flicker in Nicole's eyes hinted she knew the truth of the matter.

'It's time I left: I've things to do, and my flight leaves first thing tomorrow. Look, here's my card. Let me scribble my mobile number on the back.

NICOLE GALLISOT
Institut du Monde Arab

1, rue des Fossés-Saint-Bernard Place Mohammed-V 75236
Paris Cedex 05 – FRANCE

Ramzi slipped it into a trouser pocket. Down in the office, he tapped in the combination and gave her the Rolex, travel pouch and wallet.

'Let me give you a card too.' Ramzi rummaged about, but only found his personal card showing his name and phone number.

'It looks like we've run out of the Riad Waqi business cards. I'll scribble the riad's e-mail and address on the back of mine. Here. Now, let me walk you to a taxi. You're carrying a small fortune—'

'I'd rather you didn't. I need time to clear my head. Just point me towards the souks.'

'Are you going to blow all that cash?'

Nicole smiled. At the door, she adjusted her *Hermès* scarf, kissed his cheek and thanked him for the tea. Caught in the supernatural light that follows rain, he watched her walk away between the rose-red walls. With a quick glace back, she swept out of view. Shutting the door, he wheeled round to find Latifa, brandishing a stick of incense and a pot of salt.

THIRTEEN

'What's wrong? Is it the drains again?'

'No,' Latifa said, shaking salt over the step. 'It's that woman. Believe me, I have a sixth sense about these things. She's got the devil inside her. She'll cast a spell over you.'

'But I thought you told me to find a wife?'

She struck a match and lit the incense and wove the perfume all over him. Ramzi sneezed, and tried to wave the smoke away before she put it down by the door. Crossing to the salon he cleared away the two glasses, but Nicole had left a little tea in hers. Throwing it into the fire, it hissed.

'Monsieur Ramzi?'

It was Hisham, ready to deliver his bad news: a negative online review about Riad Waqi. Many independent travellers rated hotels and guesthouses on Trip Intelligence, so he paid little attention, because the system was easily corrupted. Some riads in Marrakech were not officially registered, but received five star ratings every other day, pushing them into the top ten. The owners either forged reviews or held their guests in a hammerlock until they cooperated. Still, a bad notice could put a ranking into free-fall, and most prospective visitors took the assessments at face value.

Like a sheep poised to face its destiny on Eid, Ramzi followed Hisham into the office. Sitting in front of the Mac, he tapped the keyboard and up came the problem.

'I booked Riad Waqi for the great riad experience and because of the good reviews it received. I now feel like some of the reviews were manipulated. My first complaint is the owner, a Mr Ramsey, who claims he is Scottish, who is highly unprofessional and to be frank, a bit stupid. He seemed bothered every time I had a question and more than once I caught him making a face and rolling his eyes. Worse still, he makes his sarcastic remarks with a smile. (It is not a language/cultural difference, which can be easily distinguished). My next complaint is that the riad is in a dodgy area called the Medina. On our second night, we arrived back by taxi. As we started to walk we saw men in doorways trying to attract our attention. We ignored them, but as we walked past a young boy about ten years old cutting up a cardboard box, he raised the knife into the air and spoke to us. He may have been making a joke, but we will never know as he spoke in French not English. We then found ourselves in the middle of a group of boys playing football in the street, and the next thing was the football hit my friend's back. A woman shouted at the boys and they ran off. That was the last straw. I cannot recommend the riad due to the vile, intimidating and unfriendly local people.'

Ramzi felt giddy.

Complaints happened, but were easily resolved. For instance, a guest had grumbled about the bed linen, finest Egyptian cotton Percale with 600 threads per square inch, so Ramzi kept a set of polyester sheets in reserve. He recalled the clients who wrote the review, a couple from Rothsey, who had booked for a week and checked out after two days to a second-rate hotel in Guéliz.

Ramzi put a hand on Hisham's shoulder and told him not to fret. He emphasized the criticism was not of him or the riad. He'd use the right to compose an owner's reply, an exercise in damage limitation. Already the first line came to mind: 'The problem with the armchair anthropologists who authored this review is that they represent a certain type of western tourist that is vile, intimidating and unfriendly to the local people—'

Then a thought occurred.

'Hisham, you haven't seen a stranger hanging round the street? I don't want another complaint from guests of some guy pushing drugs at our door. Or anyone being mugged.'

'Nobody. This is a very quiet lane.'

'Good, that's one less problem.'

Nevertheless, Ramzi's eyes felt hot. Was it the strange weather, or the events at the cemetery, or Nicole's narrative compounding the rotten review, or all things together? Blinking back tears, he asked the blank wall, 'What am I doing here?' He used to be a mover and a shaker on the scientific stage, and he'd ended up a blunderer running a B&B. He spotted his parents' phone number neatly written on a post-it beside the computer. He dialled. His mother answered. They started speaking Arabic, then switched to French. She and his father were off to a Burns supper that evening. In the past Ramzi enjoyed these occasions, but today he shuddered at the line recited as a knife plunged gleefully into a Haggis: '...and cut you up wi' ready slight—'

Unaware of his current squeamishness, his mother asked about plans for *Eid*. Ramzi murmured something but his mother chatted on. She'd arranged some *halal* lamb at Amin's in Allison Street and asked a few friends for a Moroccan meal. As she rattled off the menu Ramzi's mind roamed to the house in Glasgow, to the large square rooms, the sash bay windows, the lush garden spreading beyond. It seemed another world.

'Is there something wrong?'

'Nothing.'

'I know you. Take my advice. Get out of the city and have a day in the hills to blow away the cobwebs. That's what you used to do in Glasgow.'

'True.'

'We're very proud of you, and you should be proud of yourself. I hope you know that. You're doing the right thing. Trust a mother's instinct.'

What had prompted that? Had Ramzi missed something? Puzzled, he sent his love and said goodbye.

'Hisham?'

'What happened to the business cards for the riad? I couldn't find any.'

'Monsieur Paul took the last couple. I've

ordered new ones. I found a new printer. They're cheaper but they take longer.'

Ramzi decided not to comment. He fetched a couple of bin bags and went to Paul's room. He'd keep the suitcase. He picked up the clothes, folded them, and piled them into one of the bags. In the bathroom, he chucked the toiletries. Picking up the bottle of *Eau Sauvage*, Ramzi recalled the tears the fragrance fomented. Running over the conversation, he looked back at how Nicole evaded the question about Paul's colleague Tahar. Ramzi wondered if his father's string pulling was the only reason Paul had left Paris. Maybe problems with the marriage had surfaced, making Nicole's hesitation understandable. Paul's comment, 'I'm tired of living a lie', resurfaced.

But then, a mysterious coincidence last May: Nicole left at the same time Tahar disappeared. Ramzi wondered if the two events were linked. Why had Paul come back to Marrakech, with that large sum of money? And why had he gone to the mountains, looking for this woman Zahra Ait El Amri?

Trust a mother's instinct.

Ramzi dialled Abdelsadak, Paul's driver to the mountains. He asked if he remembered exactly where Paul had gone. He did, and Ramzi arranged to be collected after breakfast the next day.

FOURTEEN

'Knives, hatchets!'

'Skewers!'

'Butcher hooks!'

'Sticking plasters!'

'Charcoal!'

Along the lanes and alleyways, street-criers dealt in the tools of death as the festival of *Eid al-Adha* crept closer. Ramzi greeted Abdelsadak, and climbed into the old Mercedes. Abdelsadak negotiated the taxi through the fruit and vegetable sellers, between a carpenter and a motorbike repair shop, out of the tightness of the medina. Along an avenue, the red ramparts set off processions of roses until, at a palm grove, he sped south towards the snow-capped Atlas.

A verse from the Quran, gold script on green plastic, danced under the rear-view mirror. Fawn slipcovers protected the seats, and mini Moroccan rugs blanketed the floor wells. A song by Warda played, and her voice infused the air. As the purple tarmac rolled behind them, the discussion turned to the Moroccan singer Samira Saeed; Abdelsadak didn't like the various influence of jazz and *Raï* that crept into her music. Ramzi thought of a concert of the Lebanese singer Fairuz he'd seen a couple of years back, accompanied by piano, strings, horns and a sax, and mentioned aloud her famous ballad, Kifak Inta, *How Are You?* The song captured a poignant meeting of two former lovers.

'I think it's silly,' Abdelsadak said.

'I disagree. It's a great love song.'

'Love song? If you want a great love song, listen to Oum Kulsoum. No one can top her.'

On that, Ramzi had to concur. Abdelsadak switched the music and the Egyptian singer's voice disarmed them. A vapour trail scored the blue sky. By now Nicole would be in Paris. Ramzi stared from the window barely seeing the cacti hedges of Barbary Fig, the boy on a mule, or the woman in a kaftan, a baby slung on her back. Abdelsadak asked what Ramzi planned to do at *Eid*. Too weary to talk anymore, he mumbled an answer, and they continued in silence. It occurred to Ramzi that Nicole had barely asked anything about his life. But why should she when she was grieving over her husband? Or, as he reminded himself, estranged husband. But did that imply that she had found him uninteresting, or of limited intellectual worth? Ramzi tried to distract his attention as the road started winding upwards.

Driving into the foothills of the Atlas made Ramzi edgier. He yearned to rock climb. At seventeen he'd started climbing in Glencoe in Scotland, becoming addicted to the adrenaline rush. Climbing cleared the mind like a puzzle, and he would always emerge exhilarated. Ramzi's mind drifted to the last climb he made, in Gran Canaria. The name given to the ascent escaped him, but he recollected it involved tackling a rock chimney—

'Monsieur Ramzi, wake up. We're nearly there.'

A hand prodded his shoulder. Dazed, Ramzi looked out at the dreaminess of it all. Minibuses and cars lined the road in front of the riverside restaurants. On wooden bridges slung from cables, people crossed the torrent of the Ourika River to reach the walnut trees and pathways to the cascades on the other bank. Abdelsadek drove on, round a spur in the hill and parked. The village of Setti Fatma rose above them, hard against a precipice.

Out of the taxi, Abdelsadak led as they climbed the sloping lanes. Eventually he pointed to a blue entrance.

'That's where I left Monsieur Paul a week ago.'

Ramzi knocked on the door. It opened. The woman had a lined face, a tribal tattoo in the centre of her forehead, and one on her chin. She brushed down her pistachio-green kaftan and pink apron and tightened the scarf over her hair.

'I'm looking for Zahra Ait el Amri?'

'Are you from the police?'

'The police?'

'Is it about my son Tahar?'

This was not what Ramzi expected. He managed to hide his surprise. 'I think a friend of mine knew your son.'

'Come in, please.'

Abdelsadak, the soul of discretion, took his leave. Ramzi stepped into the long narrow room of a psychedelic dream: strawberry walls lined with a blue floral banquette, green cushions, a leopard skin print blanket, and a yellow kilim on the floor. In the corner, a large television stood beneath a shelf.

Ramzi took the copy of Paul's passport from

his jacket pocket and unfolded it.

'Did you know Paul Gallisot? He came here last week.'

'Why would he come and see me, sir? As far as I know he wasn't a friend of Tahar. I'm sorry if you had a wasted journey. May I offer you some tea?'

'Thank you.'

She lit a gas burner. Blue flames raced under the kettle, and a metallic bubbling soon filled the room. From a bag of moist jute Zahra teased out fresh mint. Into a silver teapot she poured a glass of water, swilled it round, and emptied it into a basin. Tea, mint and sugar cubes were put in the pot, boiling water on top.

As they sipped the tea—he expected his teeth to melt in the hot, sweet liquid—Ramzi asked when she'd last seen her son Tahar.

'Perhaps sir it might be easier if I spoke in French, and I hope I don't offend you by saying that? Tahar visited last year, and promised to return on the Prophet's Birthday. But the only visitors I had were the police. They questioned me all afternoon. They suspected he'd been involved with the Casablanca bombers last May. That's how I knew Tahar had disappeared. But sir, believe me, my son would never

113

get involved with anything like—terrorism.'

Zahra whispered this last word.

'How did Tahar get in touch with you?'

She shot an indulgent look as she pulled a basic Nokia mobile from her kaftan pocket.

'I try and phone him every day. At first, I thought he'd forgotten to charge his phone, and left a message. Then the number was disconnected.'

Taking out his own mobile, Ramzi suggested there might be a problem with her Nokia, and asked Tahar's number. As she rattled it off, he tapped it into the directory, and rung it. An operator advised him in Arabic and French that the number was unobtainable.

'Are the police still looking for him?'

'I don't know, sir. But the police took a photograph of Tahar with them when they'd left.'

'Do you still have one?'

Off the shelf above the television she took down a cedar-wood box and placed it beside her. Unlocking it she lifted out some pictures and passed two across. He tipped them towards the light from the small window for a closer view. One was of a young man standing in front of the Eiffel Tower, and the other a portrait from a photographer's studio. The chiselled face, full lips and green eyes were those of a model.

'He got to France, unlike his father.'

'Is his father here?'

'He died when Tahar was a baby.'

'I'm sorry—'

'It was a foolish thing. When we married we left Setti Fatma for Marrakech and rented a room in the medina. But after a series of dead-end jobs, my husband felt all the doors were closed in front of him here in Morocco. Soon he became drunk with plans to make a fortune in Europe. I reminded him of the proverb, "The tar of my country is better than the honey of others." But he laughed at that. "Wait till I send for you and Tahar," he said. Finally, my husband set his mind on emigrating to France.'

Ramzi recalled Nicole's comments description of the grim Parisian suburb where she grew up. He speculated if that was the same reality of Tahar's father's dreams.

'The problem was he couldn't get a visa. Instead he travelled with a friend to Tangier, and paid for a place on an inflatable raft to Spain. They planned to land at a deserted cove, and make their way over the border to France. But faced with the Strait of Gibraltar, his friend lost his nerve and dropped out. The boat left at night. I never heard of him again. I was left with our baby.'

The Strait had some of the most treacherous currents in the world. The inflatable raft, probably overcrowded, was tantamount to suicide. Ramzi was moved by the implication of her words.

'Tahar started to wake at night, crying in terror. At first sir, I imagined his cries were the screams of my husband. But someone suggested the nightmares were caused by visions of jinns. As I was still in Marrakech, I put him under the protection of the Saint Sidi Bou Amar by performing a simple ritual. At the hour of prayer, I put Tahar for a moment on his tomb, and afterwards washed his hands with water from the shrine. I put an egg in his hand, and made him throw it into the sanctuary as an offering, as I chanted, "O Great saint, we lodge a complaint against the weeper." And from that night on Tahar slept a honeyed sleep.

'I waited for my husband, but in the end returned here to Setti Fatma to be with my family. At school Tahar proved an outstanding student. A teacher compared his Arabic script to the breaths of angels. He won a scholarship to a boys' boarding school run by a religious charity, but during his holidays he earned money as a guide, leading tourists up to the fifth cataract, or higher, and picked up different languages with ease.'

Zahra rummaged in the box, and produced another photograph of Tahar, perched on a rock with a cascade of water in the background.

She smiled. 'In fact, Tahar had such charm and a reputation for his climbing ability that people came for the day and asked for "The Goat Boy."

'Well, he got his Baccalauréat and a scholarship to study engineering in Paris. What a celebration that was! I confess I feared Paris might seduce him, but refused to stand in his way. Tahar was young, yet he often criticized western values. Every year he came back with some money in hand to give me. He bought me this sewing machine and the television over there. And in time he returned to Morocco to work in Marrakech. That's why I feared the worst. Tahar used to visit every month and gave me an allowance to pay the bills. He thought I depended on this but to tell the truth, sir, I put the money aside to give back to him at his wedding. Instead I supplemented my sewing with work at one of the restaurants by the bridge.'

'You must be very proud of him.'

'Yes sir, I am.'

They sat in silence for a moment. Ramzi finished his tea and took out his wallet, but Zahra leapt to her feet.

'Sir, please take your money with you. I don't want your charity.'

'Please, you misunderstand. I only wanted to give my contact details.'

Ramzi withdrew one of the business cards printed with his name and mobile telephone number. Zahra put the card with the photographs in the cedar-wood box.

'So why are you interested if my son knew that Frenchman?'

'Paul Gallisot? He was murdered last week.'

'I see. What a terrible thing.' She locked the box and smiled. 'Thank you for coming and keeping me some company. I'll let you know, sir, if I hear from Tahar.'

Ramzi left as the call to prayer filled the plunging lanes and echoed through the valley. He found Abdelsadak polishing the hubcaps of the Mercedes. Although pleased they'd get back to Marrakech by lunchtime, he took pains to finish the job he'd started. He refused help, so Ramzi leant against a wall watching until the chrome gleamed.

As they drove back, they settled into a comfortable silence, and Ramzi turned the meeting with Zahra over in his head. He felt a strange affinity with Tahar. Ramzi reflected how his own mother left Morocco. Armed with a degree and a grant to study in Scotland, the British Embassy in Rabat surrendered a visa. At Glasgow University, she'd met his father. They married, he was born, and his mother ended up as a lauded academic. Later she took up British nationality.

He felt sympathy for Zahra. The fact Tahar's father had drowned, and Paul's mother had drowned, one trying to leave North Africa, and the other swimming towards it, seemed to fit the sides of the same equation. An absurdity that Ramzi believed tied Paul by some means to Tahar.

If Ramzi considered Tahar's disappearance, the police visits to Ingémaroc and to his mother, and the companion in the burqa, perhaps he could be linked to the Casablanca bombings. Ramzi recalled the last night at the riad and Paul's anguished look at the mention of the attack. Had he been murdered because he knew something? Perhaps he had a message, or a remittance, or a present for Tahar's mother that he never delivered? Had that been the reason for Paul having ten thousand euros in his possession? But if so, why did Paul turn on his heels?

From the newspapers, Ramzi knew enough about the way terrorist cells worked to see this as unrealistic. By confiding in Paul, Tahar compromised the larger organization, which defeated the ultimate purpose.

He considered another scenario. Guilt for some reason impelled Paul to find Tahar's mother. Yet Ramzi remained uncertain, and this made him all the more determined to discover the truth.

Ahead, above the green plain and red earth, the elegant minaret of the Koutoubia Mosque marked an invisible city. In a couple of days *Eid al Adha* would be played out as it had been for centuries. After the cull, there'd be sheepskins piled on street corners and ram's heads burning over charcoal fires in the lanes. And throughout Marrakech, the smoke, burning wool and flesh would carry the scent of death.

FIFTEEN

'This is my grandfather making the sacrifice,' Hisham said.

On his mobile, he showed Ramzi a video clip of a ram, its head hennaed and black rings painted round its eyes. And with the words, *Bism'illah* and a single slash of the knife, it went to glory in a bathtub.

But Hisham had more excerpts. Working as a team, the family soon had the head and horns roasting on a brazier, and the nozzle a bicycle pump inserted into a cut in a leg so the decapitated body could be blown up like a balloon, to separate the fleece from the carcass. After being disembowelled, a water hose was connected to the intestines to flush them out. As the finale, the poor animal was hung from a hook, and Hisham's father gave a V for victory sign.

During the afternoon Latifa bustled in.

'What a tragedy: guess what happened to my sister?'

'Is the baby OK?'

'Yes, *alhamdulilla*! But their sheep leapt off the tenth-floor balcony—'

After painting the chain of destruction caused by the kamikaze ewe, Latifa rewarded Ramzi with a plate of lamb kebabs, which he ate with a little salt, lemon juice and *harissa*. So, for another year, the excitement of *Eid al Adha* ended.

February was as void of sheep as it was of tourists, and the main excitement was the arrival of the new business cards.

'Sorry Monsieur Ramzi. Some of the letters smudged, and the cardboard is thinner. But for the price—'

'The box is huge. How many did you order?'

'Ten thousand—'

'Ten thousand!' Ramzi dropped into a chair. 'Well they should last twenty years.'

'Not if we expand,' Hisham smiled. 'We could buy out one of the neighbours, add more bedrooms, and with economies of scale—'

'Why don't you and Latifa take a short holiday?'

The news delighted Latifa as her sister was nearing her due date, and breezed off to spend a few days in Casablanca. Hisham, reluctant at first, ended up with vague plans to see a cousin in Fes.

Ten thousand business cards. Ramzi felt he had been handed a life sentence, chaining him to Riad Waqi. The drama of Paul's death and the initial intrigue surrounding it had been a welcome diversion, but now his detective work had stalled. This happened in scientific research too, but with that Ramzi could switch his attention to another problem, then return to the first. However, the prospect of a second guest being murdered appeared unlikely.

In the next days, for their few customers, Ramzi arranged airport collections, rustled up more conventional breakfasts, cleaned, and tried not to roll his eyes when assaulted him with questions. Bookings came in for the spring, and as far ahead as the autumn, so he spent a lot of time ping-ponging e-mails into the ether. But every so often he picked up Nicole's card, and studied it as if the letters contained a secret code, only to discover half an hour had slipped by as he contemplated the triad *Paul+Nicole+Tahar*.

By the time Hisham and Latifa returned—the baby was girl—all the medina's little kids turned into strolling minstrels, the lanes and alleys resonating with the pit-a-pat and rattatatto of clay drums. *Ashura* had superseded *Eid*, bringing a festival that marked two historical events: the day Noah left the Ark, and the day that Moses was saved from the Egyptians by God. And in Morocco, *Ashura* became above all, a children's celebration.

Ramzi might have forgotten the tragedy of Paul Gallisot, but for an invitation to the Galerie Windsor for a *vernissage*. The opening introduced a new exhibit of Arabic calligraphy.

The first time he visited the Gallery, the owner Peter Crum, had taken a rather snooty attitude, until Ramzi asked if he had any work by James McBey, a fellow Scot who had fallen in love with Morocco and spent the latter part of his life in Tangiers with his American wife Margueritte. Crum's manner changed. In fact, he had something from a series of etchings McBey made after his first visit to Morocco in 1912.

In the backroom, he produced a folder containing the etching, *Tangier*, a poetic and mysterious plate of the town at sunset, a caravan of Moroccans riding on donkeys along the empty beach. Ramzi delighted in the detail, the donkey bolting with its rider, and the two gunboats moored in the bay that were a reminder of the dangers at the time the French established the protectorate. Despite the price, he bought it on the spot.

The day of the *vernissage*, children were at school, giving a short break from the staccato of the clay drums. Later that afternoon, Hisham went to rendezvous with a group of eight who had booked the riad for one night, arriving by bus from the south of Morocco. Soon afterwards Ramzi heard voices and what sounded like a frog, so went down to investigate.

He walked into the courtyard and thought for a moment he'd been charged and tried in absentia as a traitor to science and here was the firing squad dispatched to administer the sentence. Six young men stood in a line, but despite the civvies, their extreme haircuts, posture and identical mountain boots distinguished them as soldiers.

Fresh-faced and British, they were nineteen, maybe twenty years old, the corporal a little older. They stood at ease whilst Ramzi asked various questions. A gruelling tour of duty over with, they were enjoying some leave before a posting to Cyprus.

'So how do you like Morocco?'

'Like where we've been,' one of the squad

said. 'We can't understand the people. By the way, is there somewhere to buy beer?'

The corporal allocated rooms and, dismissed, the soldiers dispersed around the riad. Finishing some admin in the office, Ramzi went back to the courtyard, where the young men stood around drinking tea. One of the soldiers croaked like a frog and the others chuckled. Not amused, Latifa summoned Ramzi to the kitchen.

'Look at what they've done to our towels!' she said waving a white towel that appeared to have been used to clean earth off someone's boots. Muttering a few words of condolence, he beat a retreat.

One of the soldiers *ribbited* again. 'Neil's looking for a mate!' roared one of his comrades.

Ramzi suspected the search would be long. Hard on this the first pounding of taajira drums exploded from the lane outside the riad. One of the soldiers dived to the ground. Ramzi expected a burst of Homeric laughter, but the smiles vanished. A couple of friends went and helped the young man up. Disorientated, he looked around.

'They're drums, Andy, there're only drums.'

Ramzi turned towards Corporal Shepherd. Not turning a hair, he lounged in the b'hou, pen poised over a crossword puzzle.

'An instrument almost certainly played, eight letters,' he said. 'I guess we can rule out a bass drum.'

He laughed, as did Ramzi, though he preferred the challenges of quantum mechanics to crosswords.

'"Almost" means to remove the last letter. "Played" indicates an anagram. "Certainly" with its last letter removed is "certainl" and "certainl" anagrammed gives "clarinet". Are any of my men still in the courtyard? No?'

Putting the paper and pen to one side, the Corporal explained that Andy was suffering from Post-Traumatic Stress Disorder.

'It's not surprising. Teenagers drift into Job Centres to find out about the Army. They see pictures of tanks crashing through countryside and smiling soldiers with twigs in their helmets. They don't expect the horror. But when they do experience it, it possesses them. Some soldiers cope and find a way to compartmentalize it. Others can't.'

'Like Andy?'

'Exactly. It's never easy to peel bits of a child off your combat gear and call it collateral damage. But I've met worse. Andy started vomiting and having blackouts, common signs of PTSD. All the squad could do was try to help him as best as possible. But these ghosts stuck with Andy and they won't let go.'

Ramzi flinched, and let the Corporal return to the crossword. He hoped the walk to the *vernissage* would raise his spirits, and hurried to change into a blazer. On the way, out he stepped aside as two of the squad waltzed in with a slab of Casablanca beer.

Ramzi foresaw a late night ahead. Along the lane he collided with two boys and a girl happily thumping their drums.

'*Bonjour* Riad Waqi.'

Ramzi stopped, and crouched down. 'Can I tell you all a secret? I've a sick client at the riad.'

'How sick? Is he dying?'

Ramzi put his fingers to his lips. 'Shhhh! He needs complete silence. Do you know what could kill him?' Ramzi clicked his fingers. 'A sudden sound like this.'

The little kids' eyes almost popped from their sockets.

'Or like this—' Ramzi fluttered his hands on one of the drums. The children flinched.

'So, if you keep away from the lane tonight, tomorrow I'll buy you all a bag of sweets.'

'*Inshallah*,' a boy whispered.

They skedaddled.

SIXTEEN

The twenty-minute stroll in the mild evening proved the antidote Ramzi needed. Approaching the gallery, he started to consider tackling crossword puzzles as a solution to keep his mind active. The entrance stood a few steps down from the level of the road, and the iridescence of people and paintings through the plate glass windows brightened his mood. Inside the gallery Peter Crum was holding court in the centre of the exhibition. Seeing Ramzi cross the room, he raised a flute of champagne. Ramzi nodded and, taking a glass of *Pol Roger* from an orbiting tray, went to size up the paintings. One transformed Huwawallah, *He is God,* into the outline of a boat on the sea. Another used verses from the Holy Qur'an to create a filigree mosque and minaret. Nearby a sculpture of interlocking Kufic script balanced on a pedestal.

'Clever, don't you think?'

Ramzi turned and faced Inspector Karim. They shook hands.

'Is this business or pleasure inspector?'

'Pleasure. You look surprised? Perhaps, Monsieur Ramzi, you think that policemen can't appreciate art?'

'Not at all. Crime is a form of art, isn't it?'

Inspector Karim smiled. 'It often is, but not as yet in the case of Paul Gallisot.'

'So, you have still to solve it?'

'I suppose there's no harm in telling you what we know. After all, the victim was a guest at your riad. To date, our enquiries show that Paul picked up a teenage Moroccan boy in Guéliz, on Avenue Mohamed V to be exact. Traces of body fluids were found on Paul during the autopsy, and other corroborating evidence.'

'Paul had sex with the boy?'

'That's what we suspect.'

'And have you traced him?'

'Yes.'

'Where is he? What does he look like?'

'You'll be wanting his phone number next,' Inspector Karim said. Ramzi blushed. 'But for the record, he's shorter than Paul,' the Inspector said, 'but broad-shouldered and muscular.'

'So, this young Hercules overpowered Paul

and killed him?'

'No. Not this "young Hercules" as you put it. The teenager has been released from custody.'

'How did you find him?'

'The case was solved not by art, but a cliché. The teenager witnessed the murder and returned to the scene of the crime, a lonely street with few villas. The policemen on duty challenged him almost at once. When I interviewed him, he broke down and confessed that he had met up with Paul.'

'But did he identify the murderer?'

'No. Paul left the apartment first. As a precaution, the boy left a few minutes later. When he turned the corner, he saw a man cross the road and call Paul's name. The next moment they struggled with a knife. To his credit, the boy shouted, but regretted it. Paul seemed to freeze, losing concentration. The assailant saw his chance, finished the killing, and fled. When the coast was clear, the boy ran to Paul, but all too late. Thinking he'd be blamed, he left the scene of the crime.'

'Maybe they were in it together?'

'We considered that, but after questioning, ruled it out.'

'All in all, a humiliating death.'

'I prefer to call it a foolish death. Tolerant as Marrakech may be, sex between men is still illegal. It would have been safer to find a lover or a rent-boy in Europe. And if Paul Gallisot had an inclination for young North African men, indulging these desires in France would be perfectly possible. Still, Paul knew the risks when he left the riad that evening, judging by the fact he left behind the watch and wallet. To me, that spoke of premeditation rather than to a moment of madness.'

Ramzi thought of the wad of euros Paul put aside in the safe. 'How much was the boy making? Property in Hivernage is expensive.'

'He had a pimp. A Belgian who owned a real estate agency. He rented boys as well as apartments, and had the keys to the ones that were empty. It seemed Paul met him when he moved to Marrakech looking for accommodation. Perhaps he'd used his escort services before, but that is only speculation. When we found out, we swooped, but the Belgian had already made tracks. One thing the Mayor of Marrakech does not want is the city to become a haven of sex tourism.'

'And the murder and the murderer remain a mystery?'

'Exactly. To have a motive would be helpful, but we don't. But we can't classify it as a random event, like a mugging gone.'

'Because he called Paul's name.'

'Exactly.'

'Are you certain about that? The boy wasn't mistaken?'

'We are satisfied he was telling the truth.'

Ramzi touched on the subject of Tahar. Inspector Karim kept his composure, and asked what he knew. Ramzi felt it would be ridiculous to outline his role as an armchair detective.

'I'd heard he worked with Paul Gallisot.'

'He did,' Inspector Karim said.

He looked at his watch and took his leave. Ramzi congratulated Peter Crum on the exhibition and left. Afterwards he returned towards Bab Doukkala, floodlights setting the gateways ablaze against the darkness.

Back in the medina at Riad Waqi he hoped the squad had gone clubbing, but instead they talked and laughed and croaked on the roof terrace. Ramzi found a bottle of wine, opened it, took a glass and slinked up to his room, settling into an armchair. Why had Paul come to Marrakech? For gay sex? To see

Tahar? Or to deliver a message to his mother? If so, what was the message, and why did she deny recognizing him? And why the teenager? Perhaps it explained the excitement in Paul's eyes as he left on that fateful night. Algeria lurked, a virus dormant in Paul's bloodstream. Maybe lying in the young Arab's arms transported him back to treasured moments with his friend Salem and other memories of childhood. Maybe it relieved an ache for a world free from the prescriptive pressures of adult life. And here in North Africa it satisfied a longing that an affair with a *beur* in France couldn't, a quickening of the soul that tied Paul to his roots.

Ramzi poured a second glass: he liked this Domaine de Sahari Reserve, the taste of plum, black cherry and hint of oak. As he drank he became sure Héloïse knew more than she'd let on about Paul. Maybe it concerned something with Salem, or someone later in his life.

He considered if Paul's confused sexuality might have been the reason he and Nicole split. Ramzi recalled the receptionist at Ingémaroc, saying something about Paul 'didn't ring true.'

'I'm tired of living a lie,' Paul said to Nicole. Did it refer to his father, as his wife had presumed, or to the fact he was homosexual?

More wine: let it dull the pain. Maybe it was time, Ramzi thought, to find a girlfriend. A gale of laughter rebounded from the roof. He went to bed, but both his thoughts and the soldiers' festivities kept him awake. At 3.37 precisely, the squad finally hit the sack.

He tiptoed down and put out the lights. Window partly open, the call to prayer swirled into the room, but as he floated into a fine sleep he was roused with a jerk.

A man's scream disturbed the bird calls of dawn.

SEVENTEEN

Breathless, Ramzi leapt out of bed and peered into the courtyard. By the tone of it, he prepared to referee a lager-fuelled punch-up. But he saw no sign of the squad, and the shouting subsided into moaning and weeping tempered by a voice of appeasement. In the end, he went back to bed, certain it was the young recruit with PTSD. And soon, all fell silent.

Determined to intercept Latifa's explosive arrival, Ramzi had a broken sleep. He scared her out of her wits as she found him hovering by the front door. At breakfast Corporal Shepherd came and apologized for any disturbance. Ramzi offered him coffee. As he stirred in two sugars and milk, he explained he shared the room with Andy because the young man suffered from a typical symptom of PTSD: nightmares.

A line came to Ramzi, from Siegfried Sassoon, 'Their dreams drip with murder,' but he was adroit enough not to quote it.

'What about sleeping pills? Would they help?'

'Andy prefers not to take anything. He thinks it will hurt his chances for promotion, and he's right. Anyhow, I must go and finish my packing.'

Hisham arrived with an armful of fresh roses. Before leaving, Corporal Shepherd presented two surplus packets of prosciutto bought in London for sandwiches on the squad's trek, and a few discarded magazines. Ramzi didn't eat pork, but thanked him, said a cheerful bon voyage and took the forbidden meat to the fridge. In the kitchen Latifa sat on a low stool cutting the stems of the yellow roses, and arranged them in two white vases.

Weary, Ramzi flopped on the daybed in the b'hou and flicked through the magazines, one on computers, one on golf, one on gardening, and a copy of TIME. A picture caught his attention: a full-page ad for *Eau Sauvage* cologne. Ramzi recognized the model, pulling a polo neck half across his face, as Zidane, the legendary French soccer player.

Ramzi's mind raced.

Zidane was a *beur*, the son of Algerian immigrants. At first Ramzi wondered if Paul used the same cologne because of this. As he contemplated the power of advertising, another rather wild thought struck. Perhaps Tahar used to use *Eau Sauvage*, and Paul had followed suit. This supported the idea of some sort of relationship between the two men. And yet it might also explain what prompted Nicole's apoplectic reaction to the scent: not memories of Paul, but memories of Tahar. Perhaps she discovered the two men were lovers?

The idea might be far-fetched, but the pieces fitted. He couldn't leave it at that though. Ramzi resolved to visit Bob Spasoff, Paul's colleague at Ingémaroc. Grabbing his keys, he left the riad.

At first, he thought his luck was out, as nobody replied to the bell. About to leave it for another day, an upstairs window slid open, and a man's voice called out in French.

Down at the gate, Ramzi introduced himself as a friend of Paul Gallisot.

Bob nodded, as if he expected him. 'I don't know what's happened to the receptionist. She left to buy envelopes at the kiosk around the corner, but she's been gone for two hours. I've been up and down like a yoyo answering the phone.'

'I thought she said you were American?'

'I am, but I spent part of my childhood in France. Come upstairs. Sorry to have missed Paul's funeral.'

Ramzi sensed Bob seemed nervous, and decided he might relax a bit if he switched into English.

Arriving in the office Ramzi crossed over to a blueprint taped to the wall, a plan of the *khettaras* of Marrakech. He feigned ignorance.

'This looks fascinating,' he said. 'But what are *khettaras*?'

Bob's face lit up. Pretending he didn't know up from down, Ramzi listened to an enthusiastic lecture about these underground systems of irrigation. Stretching for kilometres, they enabled the planting of the city's palm groves and gardens besides supplying adequate water to the medina. Even more remarkable, they'd been built by hydraulic engineers in the twelfth century. At present, Bob led a team surveying this ancient system, but in fact, Tahar had started the project.

'Tahar? I never met him,' Ramzi said. 'What sort of person was he?'

'I liked Tahar a lot,' Bob said. 'The guy was merry as a cricket. Darleen and I asked him for dinner one weekend, and wow, did he hit it off with the boys. When Paul arrived in Marrakech, he and Tahar roamed about like best buddies. Most weekends they'd go to a pool, or shoot off on some trip or other, sometimes to the coast, to Oualidia or Essaouira. All pretty understandable, if you factored in Paul's temporary bachelor status.'

'What happened after his wife, Nicole arrived?'

'Things cooled off between Paul and Tahar. Or so I thought.'

'Meaning?'

'Well, several months went by, and then the three of them planned a trip to the south, to see the Blue Rocks.'

'The Blue Rocks?'

'Down south in the desert: near Tafraoute. Back in 1984 a Belgian artist, Jean Vérame, picked out some rocks and boulders and spent three months with the local fire brigade plastering tons of paint over them. Shades of blue and red, purple here and there. Whether you think it is art or just plain vandalism, there's something about the place. It's weird. And I mean weird.'

'In what way?'

The gangly American seemed reluctant to say more, but Ramzi persisted.

'Did they tell you they thought the place was, as you put it, *weird*, after their trip?' Ramzi said.

'No. it was the other way round. I had already gone camping there with Darleen and the boys.'

'I see. You told them—'

'I told Paul—'

'Just Paul?'

'I don't know why I told him what happened there. We'd been on a site visit and had a few beers at the hotel.'

'Something happened there—?'

Bob fiddled with the elastic band on his pony tail.

'OK,' he said at last. 'The only person I've told this story to is Paul and now I've gone this far, I might as well tell you too. We set off to Tafraoute at lunchtime, and getting there by nightfall had been a tough drive, so after we pitched camp and had a bite to eat, we all went to bed early. Darleen fell straight asleep. I thought I'd do the same, but I was overcome by a strange sensation. I tried to put a finger on it. But I can only describe it like this. Impatience. That's what I felt out there. The desert was impatient.

'I said a prayer, unzipped the sleeping bag, and crawled outside to check on the boys. Perhaps it was the terrible silence or the isolation of the place, but I felt surrounded by something, something very real, a living presence.

'It was then I saw the flap of the boys' tent was open. To my horror, the boys had gone. Fortunately, there was a full moon, as I couldn't find the torch. For a while, I stumbled around in panic, as if it was the end of everything. But I caught sight of something in the distance, a ghostly movement. I ran to it, ran as if life depended on it. That may sound a cliché, but as it turned out it did—'

'Go on.'

'I found the boys standing together on the summit of a mammoth boulder. I can't explain how they got there. I kept calm. I called out, but in reply Jack and Stevie held hands, as if they were going to step into an abyss. There was nothing for it but to start climbing. I picked a route in the moonlight and started up. With every couple of moves I was convinced I would fall. Finally, I pulled myself onto the top, wondering what monstrous power had brought them there. Jack and Stevie still held hands, and seemed unaware of my presence. I crept up behind them and grabbed them by the necks of their T-shirts, and hauled them back from the edge.

'They didn't seem to recognize me at first. I shook Jack, I shook him hard, demanding to know why he'd left the tent.

'He said, "They told us to—"

'I said, "They? Who were they?" Jack pointed across the desert. I stared and stared, but saw no one. I turned back to the boys—'

'And?'

'It was a moment I'll never forget. They smiled in the dark, and as their teeth uncovered, and for a split second, my own sons terrified me.

'I hugged them, trying not to cry. Somehow, I managed to get the three of us down to safety.

'I'd pin it on too much sun and fresh air, or too much of the chili we'd brought for supper, or an overactive imagination. But as sure as fate, the boys weren't fooling around. Something or someone possessed them that night.

'Right after breakfast we packed up and headed back to Marrakech. We never talked about it again. As I said, Paul was the only person I told this to, apart from you.'

'After hearing this, he still arranged a trip there?'

'Exactly. Shortly afterwards, Paul said he

wanted to see the Blue Rocks for himself. He asked if he could borrow some of our camping gear for the weekend: two pop up tents and three sleeping bags, to be exact. It took me by surprise, but I agreed. I discovered the second tent and third sleeping bag were for Tahar. Maybe Tahar wanted a break too, because he'd been acting strangely for a couple of weeks.'

'Strange? How?'

'Moody. Snappy. It wasn't like him at all.'

'And did the trip go OK?'

'They borrowed all the camping gear, but in the end Paul said they didn't go. At first, I reckoned my story had put him off. But Paul blamed it on two things. First, Tahar cancelled. Second, Nicole had fallen ill. That must have been true, because she left Marrakech almost immediately afterwards, to see a doctor in Paris.'

'And Tahar?'

'Well, he didn't turn up for work that Monday. It was after the Casablanca bombings, so must have been the 19th of May. The receptionist tried to contact him, but failed. The next day the company director phoned the police; they arrived straightaway and everyone underwent questioning. As

Paul insisted they'd changed their plans and stayed in Marrakech that weekend, I hadn't mentioned the trip. But I did tell the police I thought Tahar restless and moody during the previous couple of weeks.'

'What was their reaction to that?'

'I reckon the police suspected something that crossed my own mind. Maybe Tahar's jitteriness meant he was involved. Perhaps he knew about plans for a bombing, but not the date. The date turned out to be the weekend of the camping trip, so he'd cancelled. And vanished.'

'Is that what you think?'

'Do I think Tahar was a terrorist and linked to the bombings? No. Darleen and I bumped into him once in the Rue de la Liberté. The woman with him wore a veil, the whole kit and caboodle. Darleen was a bit alarmed, but it I said it doesn't mean anything, each to his own and it is a Muslim country. It didn't make Tahar a fundamentalist or a terrorist. Besides, something puzzled me, something I never followed up.'

'And what was that?'

'I'm sorry Ramzi, but I must stop now. I need to pick up my kids from the American School. I could give you a ride though?'

EIGHTEEN

Ramzi had no idea where the American School was located, but accepted immediately. Bob snapped shut the laptop, slipped it into a satchel and locked up Ingémaroc HQ. Outside he pushed on his RayBans and opened a 4X4. On the passenger seat laid a green baseball cap, a white Ingémaroc logo embroidered on the front. Ramzi picked it up as he climbed in, but Bob took it off Ramzi's lap and tossed it into the back. A Good Friday hymn played through the surround sound as they moved off.

'That's Fairuz singing.'

'She's Lebanese. Haunting, isn't it?'

'I'd forgotten: she's an Arab Christian.'

'Did you know that a hundred years ago American missionaries used to preach in Djemma El-Fna, competing with the storytellers?'

A beguiling idea, but at the moment the only

history Ramzi had patience for was Paul's proposed camping trip.

'You said there was something you never followed up.'

'Sure. A few weeks after Paul resigned and Tahar disappeared, I'd taken Darleen and the kids off for a long weekend to the Drâa valley. What a disaster! First, I made the booboo of telling the boys the river teemed with crocodiles, but forgot to say this tip-off came from Polybius the ancient Greek. Jack and Stevie were so disappointed, but Darleen—'

'Yes, I can imagine. You were saying?'

'Right. The pop-up tents. You know the type, like a small dome. When we got to the Drâa Valley, we unzipped the bags and found eleven pegs were missing.'

'And?'

'I always counted up before packing them. I was a stickler about that. Each tent had ten pegs. One tent had seven pegs missing and the other had four. And we hadn't used them since I lent them to Paul.'

'You mean—'

'Exactly. But listen to this. We managed to pitch one of the tents. The other one could get damaged if it wasn't secured, so I decided the boys would sleep in the jeep. But as we set up camp, Darleen found that the canisters of the Campingaz lantern and the single burner stove were almost out of butane. Normally they had a burn time of about six hours, but we doubted they'd last more than a few minutes. And as sure as death and taxes I'd put in two new canisters for Paul's trip.'

The revelation came as Ramzi noticed the medina walls pass out of the picture as they sped toward the suburbs. He shrieked for Bob to pull over, but just as Ramzi jumped out, Bob called him back.

'Something else.'

'Yes?'

'Right. We'd had a New Year's Eve barbeque and I organized fireworks to let off at midnight. Paul asked if I could get some for him, to take to the Blue Rocks. He wanted Roman candles, skyrockets and sparklers. He offered to pay, but I said no. Anyhow, I'd packed the fireworks in with all the gear. But I never got them back. That always baffled me.'

'Go on.'

'The question being, when did he use them? Tahar disappeared. Nicole had been ill and went to Paris. Paul resigned soon after. Paul and Nicole lived in an apartment. If they hadn't gone on the trip to the

Blue Rocks, why didn't he return the fireworks before he left Marrakech for good? Look, I better rush, I'm late.'

Ramzi made his way back into the medina. Latifa had conjured up another artwork for lunch. Lifting the conical lid of the *tajine* revealed the bronze, yellow, and violet of chicken, preserved lemons and olives.

As he ate, Ramzi ran through the chat with Bob. Tahar's jumpiness before he vanished and association with a full-cloaked Muslim woman did not make him an extremist or link him to the Casablanca bombing. Eliminating this idea, Ramzi tried to piece together the chronicle of the trio. Paul and Nicole, who he doubted were fresh-air fiends, planned a camping trip with Tahar. They borrowed two tents and three sleeping bags, and a variety of equipment including a Campingaz lantern and stove. After the weekend, Paul returned the camping gear, and told Bob they'd cancelled their plans.

Nicole had taken ill and returned to Paris. But that raised another why? It wasn't as if Morocco was lacking in medical care, both public and private.

At the same time, Tahar disappeared.

Later, Bob discovered the missing tent pegs

and the near-empty butane canisters, which implied the camping gear had been used. But why lie?

Once again, he brooded over Paul and Tahar. Héloïse's insinuations about her brother's relationship with his boyhood friend Salem corresponded to Paul's actions the night of his murder. Had there been anything sexual in Paul's relationship vis-à-vis Tahar? So they hung out together before Nicole arrived in Marrakech—what of it?

But maybe she'd discovered Paul and Tahar *in flagrante delicto*. If that happened before the trip Ramzi doubted Paul would be organizing an intimate weekend away for the three of them. So perhaps Nicole had caught them in a compromising situation later, at Tafraoute and the Blue Rocks. She flipped. Hit Tahar or pushed him, accidental death the result.

Ramzi recalled the secondhand paperback he'd bought on North London murders—it felt like aeons ago. Back in the sixties Kenneth Halliwell grabbed a hammer and dashed out the brains of his lover, Joe Orton, after reading his racy diaries. Maybe Paul had made sexual overtures to Tahar, been repulsed, and attacked Tahar in a similar frenzy? After all, Nicole mentioned Paul was easily riled.

In either scenario Tahar's body had to be

disposed of. The Gallisots, one or both of them, buried the Moroccan deeper in the desert. After all who would find it? Still, they had to agree to a pact of silence, and that could explain Nicole's sudden departure to Paris.

In the end Ramzi felt convinced the reason underlying Paul's return to Marrakech was the visit to Tahar's mother. Either Paul hoped to make amends for some wrong Tahar had done, or to atone for some evil Paul or Nicole had done to him. Yet Ramzi felt unsure on how to proceed. He could visit the Blue Rocks, but to find what? The only person who knew the truth about the trip and also Tahar would be Nicole. Perhaps he should travel to Paris to confront her?

Ding-dong!

'It's for you, Monsieur Ramzi.' Chuckling, Hisham went into the kitchen.

Ramzi laid his napkin aside and showed up at the door. To his horror he found himself confronted by a horde of grinning children, the three kids from the previous night standing at its core. Well, he'd hoisted his own petard. Accompanied by their deafening taajira drums, he reached the kiosk to buy the sweets he'd promised. Yet, despite the *allégresse*,

Ramzi found the pounding ominous.

NINETEEN

'I'm sopping wet,' Hisham said.

Ashura had hit town. As tradition dictated, Ramzi gave *zakat*, a percentage of his income, to be distributed to the poor and needy. Clay drums were smashed or put away, and silence fell over the medina. Children received new clothes, small toys and sweets, and entering into the spirit of the day known as *Zam Zam*, called after a well in Mecca, they splashed and sprayed friends and family with water.

Which is why, when he walked into the courtyard to find Hisham standing in a puddle, Ramzi put it down to overzealous kids. He was wrong. In fact. he'd done a spot of plumbing. On one of the washbasins the cold tap had bust. The good news was he'd replaced it, the bad news was the new cold tap looked nothing like the hot tap. Hisham didn't seem to notice, but Ramzi did.

Seconds later two guests checked in who'd

booked the room for seven nights. Ramzi apologized for the oddball taps and waterlogged bathroom. In doing so, he was horrified his honeyed words and handwringing called to mind two of Dickens' characters, Uriah Heep plus his devoted mother. But, then again, one of their snippets could turn into the riad's motto— 'Umble we are, umble we have been, umble we shall ever be.' Just one problem: getting Latifa to toe the line.

Not wanting Hisham demotivated, he let the days pass until he wished the guests bon voyage to London, his left hand stuffed firmly in his trouser pocket. Closing the front door, he sprang into action. In no time Ramzi sabotaged the tap by spoiling a washer. As Latifa made up the room, she came across the irreversible trickle into the washbasin and called him at once. Acting exasperated, he insisted enough was enough and promised to buy a completely new unit.

The taps gave Ramzi a purpose. Next morning, excited as a schoolboy, he woke before Latifa's arrival. He planned to buy the unit, shoot into the souks to the Café des Épices, read a paper and linger there till lunch. He set off after breakfast to Rh'milla, along the ramparts, through Bab Doukkala and past fruit and vegetable vendors.

The tap unit chosen and paid for, Ramzi bought a copy of the Guardian Weekly and strolled through Bab Laksour towards the souks. But at the entrance to the spice market at Rahba Kedima, he got trapped in a bottleneck of tourists, stuck beside cages of tortoises and chameleons. Ramzi pushed his way through, until he reached the Café des Épices. Ordering an almond milk with a splash of orange flower water, he settled back and opened the paper. This was the life!

Inside, a photograph of a colleague from Oxford ambushed him. According to the Guardian Weekly, he had made a major discovery, having identified an HIV inhibitor, a serious step in the fight against AIDS.

Ramzi closed the paper, straightened the pages, folded it carefully and put it to one side. He stared out at woven mats and baskets, and the spice stalls hung with dried hedgehogs, snakes and owls.

He drained the almond milk, rallied a little, and tried to be positive. It hadn't been a wasted year. He had created something: Riad Waqi. He provided full time employment for two Moroccans; he supported local shopkeepers, artisans, and an accountant. But now, he had a sense of being trapped, as if he was caught in the labyrinthine twistings of the ancient medina.

Dispirited, he paid, walking doggedly home. Into the bargain he'd morphed into a Moroccan Miss Marple; next he'd take up knitting. Tears blurred the vaulted passage ahead, a black hole that pulled Ramzi on.

Sunlight brought him back to earth. He almost gagged at the stench as men in green overalls shovelled slime from the sewers into sacks. People thronged round an altercation between two women. Nearby children aimed stones at each other; one hit a forehead and bleeding, the boy ran off with a yowl. Further on a young guy sat sniffing glue from a bag. Beside him, a kitten's diseased eyes were on the point of exploding.

Ramzi found it difficult to catch his breath. He felt lightheaded, and scared. Somehow, he made it back to the riad. Turning into the lane he calmed down. He dodged a couple of kids playing football with a pomegranate. Patting his pockets, he discovered he'd forgotten his keys. He hammered the knocker against the door.

'*Bonjour* Ramzi.'

He looked up, squinting against the light. An angel waved over the edge of the roof terrace. How cruel: his time was up and he still had two bottles of 1982 Petrus and a bottle of 1963 Graham's Port put aside for a special occasion.

TWENTY

'She's back,' a tight-lipped Latifa said at the door. 'And we're out of incense.'

Nicole appeared on the stairs. They exchanged another bonjour, brushing kisses on each other's cheeks.

'What are you doing here? I thought you were in Paris.'

'I've come to wrap up the last of Paul's affairs. And where better to stay?'

'I can't remember your booking?'

'I phoned Hisham and used my maiden name.'

'Hmm. Have you had lunch?' Ramzi asked.

'That's a better greeting. What's on offer?'

'Sandwiches?'

'With delicious Moroccan bread. Perfect. I'll be back down in a few minutes.'

In the kitchen Hisham slipped slivers of

leftover soap into a milk pan on the stove. Latifa stood darkly in the corner.

'Why didn't you tell me that woman was coming?'

'I didn't know.'

'O, she's a sly one.'

Ramzi tugged plastic wrap off a plate of runny Camembert, sliced open a traditional khobz round bread and took the packet of prosciutto and butter from the fridge. As he opened the meat Latifa snatched a frying pan off the shelf.

'No need for that—'

'Are you crazy? Raw meat can kill you. That will be two deaths—'

'I know prosciutto is made from a pig's ham, but the meat is salted and hung up to dry for about a year, so it doesn't need to be cooked. Latifa? Are you OK?'

'Pig? Did you say pig?'

'Pork—'

'But it looked like beef!'

'No, pork.'

'Allah forgive me! What have I done? My aunt.'

'Your aunt?'

'I asked her for lunch and in her honour I put the other packet of the meat in the tajine.'

'When did this happen?'

'I can't believe I ate pork!' Latifa said. 'I should have known, it tasted so bad.'

'But you kept saying it was delicious!' Hisham said, stirring the milk pan.

'No, you're mistaken. It tasted bad. Oh, but my aunt is so religious.'

'But you told me your aunt said it was delicious too.'

'She only meant the vegetables. I'm sure of that—'

'Did you open a bottle of wine to go with it? "Another glass of grape juice auntie—?"' Hisham teased her.

Ramzi removed himself before Latifa became hysterical. He dodged Hisham as he poured the melted soap from the milk pan into a cookie mould, and found Nicole waiting in the courtyard.

'We'll have to go out for lunch.'

'Lead the way.'

In the gathering heat, they took a taxi to Guéliz and ate at Café de la Poste under the terrace awning. Ramzi imagined a lively lunch but there were no verbal pyrotechnics over the carpaccio of monkfish and salmon. Ramzi felt a sense of panic come over him and half-regretted the invitation. Had he lost his savoir faire?

Afterwards, they strolled along Avenue Mohammed V back towards the medina. Then, as if reading Ramzi's thoughts, Nicole said, 'Do you think this is where Paul picked up that boy?'

She knew.

'I believe so.'

Saying nothing more, they continued towards the Koutoubia Mosque. An eagle circled around the four golden balls at the top of the minaret. Ramzi felt the back of his eyes hot. He could think of nothing more to say.

The tourist busses, taxis and horse-drawn carriages that fringed Djemma el-Fna jerked him back to the present. How did Nicole feel about all of this? What was she thinking right now? What did she know?

The moment had gone. Now Ramzi felt scared to ask.

TWENTY-ONE

'The milk in this coffee tastes odd. Sort of soapy.'

Ramzi cringed. He had already faced the dog-bone shaped soap in the shower. Hadn't anyone washed out the milk pan? There were no other guests, and Nicole joined him for breakfast. As they finished the fresh yoghurt, bread, jam, honey and dried dates, they spoke amiably enough, but Ramzi felt as uncomfortable as at lunch the day before.

Nicole set off to a local tailor to collect a Moroccan tunic she'd seen the previous afternoon, and left to be altered. Ramzi took a second black coffee to the salon and considered whether he should confront Nicole to know the truth. Hisham interrupted his thoughts, armed with a pile of receipts and invoices to take to the accountant. Seizing the opportunity, Ramzi thanked him for all his ingenious economies, but suggested it might be time to accept he'd reached the end of the line so far as cost-saving was concerned. *Tout au contraire.* Hisham's next ruse was to slash the electric bills by installing solar power, and he whipped out a scary looking spreadsheet. The doorbell came to the rescue.

Ramzi went to open it, expecting Nicole. But the woman at the door wore a kaftan and headscarf, and a tribal tattoo marked her forehead. It took him a moment to comprehend who it was. Standing before him was Tahar's mother.

'Sir, I have news of my son.'

Ramzi showed her in, offering her a glass of mint tea, which she accepted. He led her to the *b'hou*. She sat, gazing across the courtyard.

'Sir, is this the riad that the young Frenchman stayed in before he was killed?'

'Yes, it is,' Ramzi said.

Latifa appeared with the tea, at which point Zahra announced that she'd been to a *shuwafa*, a psychic, called Lalla Meriyum. Latifa nearly dropped the tray.

'She is very famous!'

Famous or not, it alarmed Ramzi. He understood Zahra's desperation. But a famous *shuwafa* would not come cheap. In the past, he often watched a popular American TV show, 'Psychic Detectives', where in real life, the police called in psychics to help trace missing persons, solve crimes, or get to the bottom of mysterious deaths. Handling items of clothing, photographs, or a personal possession was often enough for a psychic to point investigators in the right direction.

So, what Zahra had to say intrigued him. Ramzi poured the tea and she dropped sugar cubes, one after another, into the glass, the spoon clinking as she stirred.

'I caught the early bus from Setti Fatma yesterday, and stayed with an old friend of mine in Marrakech. Before I arrived, she made a couple of enquiries and, without explaining why, helped arrange a meeting with Lalla Meriyum. Only when I was shown into her salon did I tell her that I wanted news of my son. I said this without revealing his name, but I handed her a photo. At once the *shuwafa* recited the beginning of the twentieth *sura* of the Qur'an: "*Ta ha*. It was not to distress you that we revealed the Qur'an, but to admonish the God-fearing. It is a revelation from Him who has created the earth and the lofty heavens, the Merciful who sits enthroned on high."

'When she said this, I praised Allah. By revealing the origin of Tahar's name, the *shuwafa* convinced me she could help.

'She asked about his past. I recounted the story of the sanctuary of Sidi Bou Amar. Do you remember, sir? It's where I took Tahar when he'd been a child and frightened at night by visions of jinn. After I told her this, Lalla Meriyum decided to spend the night in the cemetery beside the shrine of Sidi Bou Amar. My neighbour and I went with her. She filled the palm of her right hand with tar and chanted various incantations. We then left her to meditate till dawn.

'As you may imagine, sir, I barely slept. I rose with the muezzin calling the dawn prayer, and hurried to the cemetery. But it was still the morning twilight, and I had to wait for the sunrise before she could study the tar—'

Zahra faltered. Ramzi laid a hand on hers. Whilst he waited for her to go on, the front door clicked. Nicole walked into the courtyard. The two women looked at each other and exchanged good mornings in Arabic, before Nicole made her excuses and retired to her room.

It was clear to him, until that moment, Zahra and Nicole had never met. Yet he barely had time to dwell on this as Zahra continued her tale.

'At first, the tar in her palm shone in the sun like a mirror, but after a short time it fell in shadow. Lalla Meriyum studied it and as I watched she went into a trance. She told us she was like a bird and as she flew she looked down between the high walls of an alleyway and there, lying on the ground, she saw a dead man—'

'And did she recognize the man?'

'The man was my son, Tahar.'

Ramzi expected tears from her, but instead she seemed to be in a sense of poignant resignation. Any words of comfort now would be mere platitudes.

'Do you believe what the *shuwafa* told you?'

'I feel it, sir. I feel Tahar has gone.'

It was a mother's instinct, a powerful force of its own, beyond that of any psychic.

'Is there anything I can do?'

'No sir, thank you. I came, sir, out of courtesy.'

They drank the tea in silence. A few minutes later she stood, straightened her scarf and kaftan, and he showed her out.

As Ramzi closed the door, Nicole rushed down the stairs, sitting on the daybed beside him, to show the tailor-made tunic she'd bought in the souks, beautifully cut, black, with small red silk buttons. Whilst Ramzi admired it, she fiddled with the Tuareg amulet round her neck.

'Who was the visitor? An old girlfriend?'

'That was Tahar's mother. She had news of her son.'

Nicole gave a low cry. In the next instant, she stared at Ramzi with a blank and rigid face. Something similar had happened when they found the *Eau Sauvage* cologne in Paul's room, so expected her to come round. Three or four minutes ticked by, but she didn't move. He wondered if she was conscious at all.

'Hisham! Latifa!'

The three of them laid Nicole on the daybed. Her limbs seemed heavy, almost waxy, and lifeless. Latifa took off Nicole's shoes, plumped up a pillow, and covered her with a duvet. She tried to give Nicole water to drink, but the liquid dribbled from her mouth. Ramzi prayed the moment would pass, but over the next hour her pulse barely registered. The cold, almost clammy skin became so pale she appeared to melt into the pillows.

The thought Nicole might die terrified him. Taking her to a hospital would be difficult; in this delicate state, the move could finish her. If he called an ambulance she might have rallied by the time they arrived. In the end, he asked Latifa for Dr Rashida's phone number, but she had no record of it. Instead, he dispatched Hisham to her surgery to ask if she could come at once.

TWENTY-TWO

About half an hour later a scooter puttered to a stop outside. Ramzi hurried to the door. As Hisham showed Dr Rashida in, his heart skipped a beat. Caught by surprise, he recalled she was married. He opened his mouth as if to say something, then closed it again.

She raised an eyebrow. 'I thought it was a guest with the problem? Could you please explain?'

'It is a guest. A young widow, Nicole Gallisot. Her husband was murdered in Marrakech a few weeks ago. She came back to visit. She's had some sort of seizure.'

'Did it come suddenly?'

'She gave a cry and—'

'Was it a cry, or did she shout something out? A word or a phrase?'

'A cry, just a cry.'

'I'd like to see her.'

Entering the *b'hou*, Nicole looked lifeless. Dr

Rashida sat on the daybed, put her doctor's bag on the low table, and flicked the locks. Out came an infrared digital thermometer she clicked and read close to Nicole's forehead. Unclipping an ophthalmoscope, she leaned over her. Her thumb lifted one of Nicole's eyelids, and she squinted through the lens. Next Dr Rashida disentangled a stethoscope to listen to her lungs and heart. She tugged it away from her ears, preoccupied. Taking a reflex hammer, she gave small perpendicular taps to Nicole's limbs. Examination over, she carefully replaced the equipment.

'Does she have a history of epilepsy?'

'Not that I know of.'

'Did she have a heavy fall? Or a blow to the head?'

'No.'

'Can you think of anything else?'

'Well—'

'Yes?'

'A few weeks ago, we were in her late husband's room here at the riad, sorting through his things. She smelled his aftershave, and had a similar reaction.'

'And what triggered this episode?'

'I told her that a woman who visited me earlier was the mother of one of Nicole's friends who disappeared. She had news of him.'

'Hmm: the two responses sound similar. Do you know if she takes any medication?'

'Again, I'm sorry I don't.'

'May I see Madame Gallisot's room?'

Ramzi led Dr Rashida across the courtyard. In the bathroom, she checked her toiletries and wash bag. Ramzi gave a shiver as he recalled searching Paul's room the morning after he was murdered. They found no medication except for a packet of aspirin and none of the pills had been popped.

'What's the verdict, doctor?'

'I could try to give a medical term for her condition. For instance, catalepsy is related to a trauma or shock. But—'

'Go on?'

'It might seem a little fantastic, but experience tells me that she's afflicted by some jinnee.'

Ramzi gave a small laugh. 'Now you're teasing me again.'

'You do know that in Arabic, the word 'jinn' has the same root as the verb to go mad?'

'The point being?'

'In modern psychological terms the jinn is our own subconscious. It represents our fears, or sometimes hidden traumas. What we must do is know them, and transcend them.'

'And?'

'I'd like to hold an exorcism as soon as possible.'

'But—'

'The practice is quite ancient and part of the belief system of many religions, including Christianity. In fact, the New Testament included exorcism amongst the miracles performed by Jesus.'

'Do you need a priest? Tell me the denomination and I'll run round to the pharmacy.'

'This is a serious matter, Monsieur Ramzi. I must contact a Grand Master, his Gnawa musicians and an assistant to help with the ceremonial rituals.' She opened her mobile and dialled.

Kicking himself for the asinine joke, Ramzi turned to the matter in hand. He recollected the film The Exorcist and the battered priest who fought the devil to save the soul of the teenage girl as her body went into convulsions and her voice became demonic, spewing curses and obscenities. In particular he remembered the scene where the girl's head started spinning like Ixion's wheel—

With her troupe of Gnawa, Dr Rashida might not be able to match this tour de force with Nicole. On the other hand, the way she equated the idea of being affected by a jinnee with the mental disorders of medical science intrigued him. With regard to the 'hidden trauma' Ramzi was certain she was on the right track, and he bet it would be related to the trip Nicole made with Paul and Tahar, south to the Blue Rocks near Tafraoute. The realities of what happened might be revealed.

All in all, what harm could come from it?

TWENTY-THREE

'I want to inform you, Monsieur Ramzi, I've invited my aunt and a couple of neighbours.'

'Perfect, Latifa! Maybe we can charge admission?' Hisham said.

Ding-dong!

They jumped. Ramzi left them, a sick feeling gripping the pit of his stomach. At the door stood Dr Rashida. He waved her in. Behind her, from the half-light, a filigree-sound of clinks and tings followed. In its centre was a tall woman, swathed in an indigo mantle. A red veil decorated with silver coins concealed her face.

'Monsieur Ramzi: I'd like to introduce the Arifa, who is the attendant of the Grand Master.'

Courtesies exchanged, the woman laid down a large leather bag and removed her cloak. Beneath it she wore a green silk jellaba embellished with tiny bells. Bangles decorated her wrists and ankles. Swishing towards the *b'hou*, her trinketry enveloped her in a silvery aura. Half-hypnotized Ramzi followed, but Dr Rashida shooed him away as they planned to dress Nicole in a loose white kaftan.

Soon afterwards Latifa's guests arrived. They looked at Nicole: one of them screamed, and two others hugged each other. The doorbell rang a third time.

'The Grand Master is here,' Latifa said.

A man with a red cap sprouting ostrich feathers, wearing a tunic as black as his skin, walked into the courtyard carrying a *ginbri*, a traditional string instrument. Hot on his heels came the Gnawa musicians with double-headed drums, tambourines and castanets.

Dr Rashida greeted the Grand Master, and led him to Nicole.

'In the name of God, the Almighty, the Merciful!'

As he invoked God, Nicole's left hand moved. Ramzi thought this promising, but Dr Rashida and the Grand Master shook their heads.

'The left hand: it confirms that she's possessed by a jinnee.'

Of course, Ramzi saw their reasoning. In Islam, the dwellers of Paradise are known as the 'companions of the right hand,' whilst those in Hell are sometimes referred to as 'the companions of the left hand.'

Losing no time, Latifa and Dr Rashida arranged cushions between two orange trees facing Nicole in the *b'hou*, and the Grand Master settled onto them. In front of him, the Arifa opened her bag and set up three candles, one red, one green, one white, and lit the wicks. An incense burner, two bowls, and some dates were removed from her bag. She arranged these on a copper tray, placing the dates in one bowl whilst the Grand Master called to Latifa to bring milk to fill the second. As the Arifa fanned the charcoal in the burner, Latifa's aunt arrived with her own retinue.

The Arifa threw incense on the coals and fumigated the *ginbri* of the Grand Master and percussion instruments of the Gnawa musicians. Scented clouds filled the courtyard. Sneezing, Ramzi retreated upstairs.

A hollow sound echoed through the riad as the Grand Master struck a few notes on the three strings of the *ginbri*. This kicked off a stale thudding of drums and a jangle of tambourines.

On the roof terrace, Ramzi leant over the parapet facing the *b'hou*, to keep an eye on Nicole. Dr Rashida joined him. Below, the Grand Master took the incense burner and, with a sweeping gesture, saluted the four cardinal points. Afterwards, to Ramzi's surprise, he took the bowl of milk and poured some of the white liquid on the ground. Dr Rashida explained the smoke attracted the jinn, and the milk was an offering.

'Brandy might be more effective.'

Dr Rashida shot him a withering look. Ramzi asked whether the spirits could harm the Gnawa. Here, Dr Rashida gave a nod of approval.

'It's a good question. In fact, the Gnawa have a needle in their hair that frightens the jinn and protects them from entering their bodies.'

At that, Ramzi almost stopped the proceedings. All this was irrational, and not compatible with science. Yet, irrationally too, as he glanced at Dr Rashida, he remained silent.

With tings and jingles, the Arifa took the bowl from the Grand Master and rubbed the rest of the milk on the *ginbri*, drums, tambourines and metal castanets. The Grand Master took up the *ginbri*. His eyebrows knitted with determination as his fingers coaxed curious rhythms from the three gut-strings. As the bass notes bounced round the courtyard, the musicians rushed from the crowd towards him. Striking their instruments, they danced, stepping in tight circles, bodies swaying.

From behind her veil, the Arifa let out a piercing quaver. Ramzi almost fell back from the parapet. Dr Rashida laughed, and he felt embarrassed. Recovering, he saw the Arifa combing Nicole's hair.

'That's how the jinn will finally escape: through the hair,' Dr Rashida explained. 'Or so tradition has it.'

Finger and thumb skipping between the strings, the Grand Master played on. The throbbing and pounding of instruments rocked the courtyard. Overhead, the stars pulsed in the night.

A crash from the percussion heralded a break in the music. But the silence was cut by the Grand Master singing over and over in a screechy voice, 'Come little friends we only wish good and everyone is well disposed towards you. Come little friends we only wish good—'

The hairs rose on the back of Ramzi's neck. The Grand Master returned to the strings of the *ginbri*, a cue for the drums and castanets to recommence.

The Arifa placed her hands a short distance above Nicole's head, undulating them downwards and over the length of the body. Nicole moaned, and started to pull herself up on the mattress.

'Ulululul—' Triumphant, the Arifa threw more incense on the burner. The clouds floated like spirits through the courtyard. Taking the dates and the last of the milk she scattered them over the ground.

'They are offerings of food to all the jinn present and to the company,' Dr Rashida said. 'A friendly spirit will be drawn into every person present, which will help draw out the evil jinnee.'

But as Dr Rashida spoke the scene turned into delirium. One of the neighbours crumpled to the ground, weeping. Another began tearing at her hair and body, and Latifa's aunt ran round and round twisting her hands together. In the middle of this, Nicole struggled to her feet and the Arifa helped her cross the courtyard.

'Is she alright now?'

'No, the jinee is still fettered.'

'Ulululululululul—'

Putting the *ginbri* aside, the Grand Master stood. As the percussion stopped, he shouted an incantation. Ramzi recognized it from the Qur'an, *sura* 114, *Al-Nus*, 'I seek refuge in the Lord of men, the King of men, the God of men, from the mischief of the slinking prompter who whispers in the hearts of men; from jinn and men.'

Nicole howled. The night snapped and her body concertinaed to the floor.

'Oh my God, what's happened?'

'She has been delivered,' Dr Rashida said with a smile.

TWENTY-FOUR

Propped on pillows in her room, Nicole sat in bed, Dr Rashida perched on the mattress beside her. Ramzi took it as a sign to leave, but Nicole called him back.

'Tahar? Where is he? What did his mother say?'

'I'm sorry, Nicole. His mother's certain he's dead.'

The doctor clasped Nicole's hand. Ramzi expected tears, but there were none.

'When did you last see him?' he said.

'The trip we went on—'

'To the Blue Rocks?'

'You know?'

'Only that you planned to camp there.'

'It was Tahar's idea. A terrible idea.'

'Why so terrible?' Dr Rashida said.

'From the start, everything went wrong. That

morning I woke up with a splitting headache. Even a couple of aspirin didn't help. Tahar met us at our apartment, and we set off. But even before leaving Marrakech, he remembered he'd left a backpack with his stuff in our kitchen. Paul had to turn back, and let Tahar run up to fetch it.

'We set off again. But things began to happen—'

'Things?' Dr Rashida said.

'Omens, call them omens. We were barely in the foothills of the Atlas, when out of the blue a donkey and cart bolted across the road. Paul jammed on the brakes and we missed them by a hair's breadth. I wanted to go back to Marrakech there and then, but Paul laughed it off, and insisted we continue. But there was worse to come.'

'Go on.'

'Paul pulled into a café near the Tizi-n-Test and parked by a truck. Tahar walked off to light a cigarette, and I called Paul aside. I begged him to return. I told him how my head throbbed and that I felt nauseous. He put it down to the altitude and the switchbacks up the mountain. He pointed out we'd put the worst of the drive behind us and the descent would be easier.

'I had no energy to argue. We went in the café and ordered mint tea. At the next table I noticed two men glancing in our direction, muttering between themselves. But they settled the bill and left. Tahar had been very quiet, and Paul, I remember, tried to kid around with him, but he barely raised a smile.

'Paul paid. Tahar followed me out. The men stood by a truck. But as we neared the jeep one of the men said something I didn't catch. But Tahar—Tahar spun round. "Say that again!" he said.

'The guy refused. Tahar strode towards him, and knocked the man to the ground—'

'There was a fight?' Dr Rashida said.

'I've gone over what happened next countless times, and I think it happened like this. The man got back to his feet, throwing a fist at Tahar, but Tahar dodged it. The second guy jumped from the cab. Tahar threw two more punches, but the man carried Tahar against the truck, hitting into his belly and chest over and over until Tahar slunk to the ground. The first man aimed a sideways kick, then spat in our direction, and both men got into the cab. The truck drove off, back in the direction of Marrakech. Tahar hauled himself up. Paul—he must have been standing there, watching—tried to help, but Tahar shook him off.'

'And then what happened?'

'I shouted, "Why did you hit him Tahar? Why did you have to do it?" I could only imagine what the truck driver said to Tahar. Paul hovered in the background, and tried to redeem himself by examining Tahar's hand.'

'Was it injured?' Dr Rashida said.

'I don't know how, but maybe because Tahar delivered the first blow, the man's teeth had taken the skin off his knuckles. We'd forgotten to pack first aid. That alone made me nervous. But Tahar laughed it off, and again, Paul insisted we go on.'

'And you did?' Ramzi said.

'Oh yes. Already that day I felt I didn't know Tahar at all. Well, after we crossed the Atlas we hit a wall of fog. We slowed down, but in the headlights a dreadful shape ran out of the mist. Paul swerved, but too late. We heard a squeal. We got out of the jeep. By the road was a pack of wild dogs. Paul had run over one of them. It lay on the road, crushed.

'Out of the blue, Tahar said we could have hurt a jinnee, and if we had, it would want revenge. In the past, Tahar told me his mother was superstitious, but I never thought he was so gullible too. Angrily, I dismissed it as nonsense. But he said the jinn had fluid bodies and could take the form of cats or dogs. In fact, people could never be sure if an animal was real or a double from the subterranean world. Believe me, I was shocked.'

'What did you do?'

'I said we couldn't leave the dog and I tried to lift it. I could see the other dogs, their jaws and eyes closing in on me. Slowly. Then, I heard growling. One dog was down ready to spring. I yelled at Paul and Tahar to do something. Paul threw a rock towards them and they backed away. He came and dragged the carcass to the side of the road. Tahar did nothing.

'We drove off with the dogs barking as they briefly chased the jeep. I just wanted the journey to end. My head was splitting, and my back aching. I wondered if I had flu or some virus, or if it was simply stress. After the incident with the dogs, it was a relief when the fog lifted. But as we drove on the sky seemed like raw clay pressing down on us. And the landscape looked so desolate that I felt as though that wilderness would somehow devour us.

'We turned south towards Ighrem, and stopped there to stretch our legs. Tahar offered to take over the rest of the way. Paul tossed him the keys. I insisted on staying in the front. We set off following the signs to Tafraoute. But my stomach churned at the sight of Tahar's right hand on the wheel. The knuckles were raw and septic.

'The road started well, but soon narrowed and broke into potholes. Tahar skirted the first few, but gave up and started driving straight through them, bouncing us about so violently that my seat belt locked.

'I told him to stop, but by then we'd reached a level stretch of tarmac. But just as I relaxed, Paul suggested rather than loop round to the Blue Rocks via Tafraoute, we go off-road, cutting straight across the wasteland. I was against it but Tahar thought it a good idea, out-voting me.

'We lurched off into rougher and rougher terrain. The jeep jolted as if any minute it'd be torn apart. Time after time I was thrown against the windows and the roof, and at times I thought my spine would be broken. I shouted to Tahar to slow down. But he said he was barely doing twenty and we ploughed on, into one soft hollow after another. And surrounding us in every direction were colossal boulders.

'Then, without warning, Tahar slammed on the brakes and the jeep slithered across the ground to a stop. I undid my seat belt, opened the door and ran. But despite the heat I felt cold—'

'Cold?'

'Yes, so cold, I started to shiver.'

'Where were you?' Ramzi asked. 'At the Blue Rocks. We had done that entire journey to see a landscape painted in pastels. It looked so absurd I almost wept. But there was something else. I felt that we were not alone. I tried to persuade Paul to leave. I offered to drive.'

'Did he agree?' Ramzi said.

'If only he had. He said, "Did you really want to travel all the way back over the Tizi-n-Test in the dark?" I said we could still make it to Agadir on the coast and spend the night at a hotel. But he refused to listen, and we drove round to find a campsite. At last Tahar pulled up in the lee of a boulder. Paul and Tahar cleared the ground and put up the tents. I wasn't well. Besides the headache and the back pains, I felt cramps in my stomach, like strong period pains.'

Nicole's voice began to tremble. Dr Rashida stroked her arm.

'Go on.'

'Paul set off with Tahar to explore. They asked me along but I said no. I was glad to be alone. Yet very quickly, an ominous feeling crept over me. My vision blurred. I looked at a trail of clouds massed across the sky. They were clouds, but I didn't see clouds. I saw faces, the faces of dead children pressed against the glass of heaven.

'I felt scared, wanting to catch up with Paul. But I had stabbing pains in my stomach. I grabbed some tissues from my bag in the jeep, and dashed to a niche in the rocks. And then—'

'Take your time—'

Nicole swallowed. 'I saw blood. And in the palm of my hand, lay my baby.'

TWENTY-FIVE

'A miscarriage. I'm so sorry,' Dr Rashida said, breaking the silence.

Ramzi reeled from the story, trying to think of something suitable to say.

'But you had no idea you were pregnant?' Dr Rashida said.

Nicole shook her head. 'My periods always had been irregular.'

Dr Rashida nodded. 'Were there any complications? There is always a risk of bleeding and infection afterwards.'

'I knew that. That's why, when we returned to Marrakech, I caught the first plane to Paris. At Orly airport I took a taxi straight to the emergency service at the Hôpital Hôtel-Dieu near Nôtre Dame. But the miscarriage was complete.'

Dr Rashida appeared satisfied.

'How did Paul react?' Ramzi said.

'Paul? He never knew. To cover it up, I told

him my period had come.' At that Nicole turned her face away, unable to hide the tears.

A silence hung over the room. Then Ramzi said softly, 'Once a man asked the Caliph Abu-Bakr, "What say you on the death of a parent?" The Caliph replied, "More property." The man posed a second question. "What say you on the death of a spouse?" The Caliph answered: "A new wedding." "And on the death of a brother?" "A cropped wing." Finally, the man asked, "And what say you on the death of a child?" The Caliph replied, "An ache in the heart impossible to overcome."'

Gently, Nicole's thumb stroked the pillow. Dr Rachida looked at Ramzi, surprised.

'I'm sorry,' Ramzi said, red-faced.

'No, don't apologize. Madame Gallisot, please try and rest. I'll return first thing tomorrow.'

Outside, the Grand Master, the Arifa, musicians and spectators had vanished into the night.

'Isn't it odd she didn't tell her husband, Paul?'

'Not necessarily. Suppressed grief is common after a miscarriage. The trauma is thrust down into the secret recesses of the memory, to wait for a safe time and place to emerge. Like now.'

'Now that Paul is dead?'

'Perhaps.'

'Well, doctor, you must get home to your own husband,' Ramzi said.

Dr Rashida laughed. 'What makes you think I'm married?'

Ramzi glanced at her hand, but saw no ring.

'I thought I saw a wedding ring?'

'I only wear it at the surgery. It stops my patients trying to marry me off. Perhaps Monsieur Ramzi, it's rather like the fact you're an eminent British scientist, but pretending to be a Moroccan running a riad? What are you trying to escape from?'

'How did you know?'

'I have my sources.'

'Well, I can't thank you enough for what you did here tonight.'

'That's a compliment, coming from you Monsieur Ramzi.'

Ramzi showed the doctor to the door. Rattled by the evening and the conversation with Dr Rashida, he poured a glass of wine. Feet up on a banquette in the salon, he half-imagined Paul beside him as he sat talking in the room a few weeks ago. The more Ramzi discovered about his life, the more he found it heart-breaking.

Ramzi recalled the scene at the cemetery after Paul's funeral, when they passed the children's graves and Nicole let out a sob. Now he realized the stab of pain she must have felt.

He considered Nicole's account of the trip. There were questions still to be answered. Why hadn't she told Paul about the miscarriage? Was it possible he wasn't the father? Yet, as Paul had no idea she'd lost a baby, how did she justify jumping on the first flight to Paris? And what of Tahar? What she had said ruled Tahar out of any involvement in the terrorist attacks in Casablanca last May as the miscarriage happened the exact same day. What had happened to him?

Ramzi recalled the vision of the *shuwafa*, who imagined Tahar lying dead in some alleyway, but putting skepticism to one side, the location made no sense. If he had been murdered in a town or city, the body would have been discovered and the mystery over his disappearance solved a long time ago.

Increasingly, Bob Spasoff's tale about his sons and Nicole's own sense of a presence, something malign, in the desert chilled the blood. What happened to Tahar lay at the Blue Rocks—of that he was certain.

TWENTY-SIX

The first person who came into Ramzi's mind the following morning was Dr Rashida. Why had she bothered to check out his background? And what was the nature of her interest? He smiled for a moment, and then he jumped out of bed, showered and dressed. Down in the courtyard his confusion doubled when he found Dr Rashida waiting to have breakfast with him.

'How is Nicole?' he asked.

'She's much better. We talked some more about what happened. Nothing confidential.'

He noticed Dr Rashida also drank her coffee black, no sugar.

'What did she say?'

'She talked more about the miscarriage. The poor woman seems to think it was some sort of retribution for looking down on childhood friends in Paris, on all the women who just wanted babies. In fact, she convinced herself she was not a proper woman. She'd conceived a baby, but let it down. Of course, I tried to explain that miscarriages often happen because the body is rejecting something that is not quite perfect.'

'But when she realized what had happened, in the desert?'

'She chose an Arabic name for the child. Walid, meaning newborn.'

'And what—what did she do with—with—?'

'With Walid? She buried him in an unmarked grave as is the custom. She used her white blouse as a winding sheet. She collected some stones to make a cairn over the top. And she recited *al-fathia*, the Exordium of the Qur'an.'

'I see. She gave the child a name and buried him.'

'Yes. That makes it easier to accept. The child was real, and the death was real.'

'I see.'

'Anyhow, thank you for breakfast. If I could make one small comment?'

'Please do.'

'I expected the coffee to be better.'

Hisham sauntered through, bearing forty long

stemmed red roses, in two bundles. To help out, Ramzi took one.

Dr Rashida smiled. 'Are those for me?'

Flustered, Ramzi handed her the flowers, much to Hisham's horror.

'If you need me, call. Madame Gallisot said she plans to rest today, maybe take in some sun on the roof terrace. But I suggest you take her out this evening, to see people. She needs to restore normal contact with her fellow human beings.'

On reflection, Ramzi decided the intimacy of a restaurant might overwhelm Nicole, so that evening he proposed they ate at the stalls at Djemma el-Fna. As they arrived, the scene resembled a storm. Moroccan flutes moaned and whistled. Drums thundered and raged from all directions. Cinereous clouds surged through the streaming light of the food stalls. Only the distant minaret of the Koutoubia Mosque, held in the flood lamps, stood steady and true.

Ramzi guided Nicole between the counters of salads, kebabs, roasted sheep heads and carts selling snails, to number 27. A waiter dressed as a sailor laid paper mats on long tables. A group of customers shifted along the bench to make room for them at the end. The waiter brought hot tomato paste and bread. They ordered meat and vegetable kebabs and roasted aubergine, and a bottle of *Oulmès* sparkling mineral water. The time passed quickly as they made small talk and absorbed the atmosphere of the square after dark. The chef twirled knives and juggled onions above a tray of red-hot coals. A kid offered kinetic toys that flared and danced like Catherine wheels. Another lad made them leap up from their seats as he threw a wooden snake in their direction. Finally, Ramzi asked for the bill. The waiter scrawled it on the paper mat. Ramzi took out his wallet.

'Bonsoir, Madame Nicole.'

Ramzi looked up at the man who spoke. He held a small girl with beads woven in her hair, and at their side stood a woman in a headscarf and kaftan. Nicole seemed to know the Moroccan instantly, but it took Ramzi a few seconds longer to place him as Abdul Majid, the concierge of the apartment block by the Majorelle Gardens.

To Ramzi's astonishment, Nicole snatched the wallet from his hand and said, 'What do you want? Money?'

Pulling out notes of one hundred dirhams, she threw four or five of them at Abdul Majid. Ramzi deemed it lucky the credit cards didn't follow. The small girl started crying. For a few seconds Abdul Majid looked scared. But in the next instant he managed to smile, apologized for interrupting their meal, and offered his condolences over Monsieur Paul.

Abdul Majid, the girl and the woman were swallowed by the crowd. Shaken by Nicole's reaction, Ramzi recovered the wallet and scrambled round on the ground retrieving the money. A silence fell between them. The waiter returned and he paid. Walking to the tea stalls, they drank glasses of *hunja*, spicy cinnamon tea, with a slab of ginger cake. Nearby, people amused themselves at the edge of a wide chalk circle, trying to hook bottles of Coca Cola with a rod and string. Others wandered about or sat cross-legged watching the performers.

'Let's see what's up,' Ramzi said.

They walked further into the throng and stopped at a circle where two young men had strapped on boxing gloves.

'Tell me boys, why do you want to box?'

'Because—'

'Look, boys shouldn't fight. But if you must you should do it cleanly and fairly.'

'Waha.'

'Start when I ring this bell. No, hold it there!'

The ringmaster addressed the crowd.

'They call themselves young men, but they look like a couple of brides on their wedding night! Let's talk about stance. Look boys, stand with your legs a shoulder-width apart and your rear foot a half-step behind the lead foot. That's right. The lead fist is the left fist and held just in front of the face. No higher, at eye level. *Waha!* Now, the rear fist is held beside the chin. Keep your elbow against the ribcage to protect the body. Do you know what causes knockouts? A punch to the jaw, so keep your chin tucked into the chest to avoid your opponent's punches. Right, start when I ring this bell. No, hold it there!'

'What? Their gloves haven't even touched!' one of the audience said.

'I forgot! Let me tell you about the hook. The punch must be thrown with the lead hand, round like this, in a semi-circle, into the side of the opponent's head—thwack!'

Then, like a blow to his own head, Ramzi remembered Nicole's account of the fight on the way to the Blue Rocks. How tactless. Mortified, he faked a laugh. 'I'm sure you've guessed. The boys never do start boxing. Nicole?'

Without a word, Nicole turned and navigated through the multitudes. With a sigh, Ramzi tagged behind into the empty souks. He mulled over the encounter with Abdul Majid, trying to recollect exactly what he said at the first meeting, just after Paul's murder. 'Well she gave me money too. I helped her, and she helped me.' That was it! Then Nicole said after Paul's funeral, 'Abdul Majid! He's never there when you want him and always there when you don't—'

Now he wondered: had she been blackmailed?

Back at Riad Waqi, Ramzi saw a chink of light below the door of Nicole's bedroom. He decided not to disturb her, even though his mind raced over what secrets Abdul Majid might have threatened to reveal.

TWENTY-SEVEN

'Monsieur Ramzi! It's an emergency!'

Stirring from a dreamless sleep Ramzi looked at the time. Ten o'clock! Good God, he'd gone to pot! Pulling on some clothes he opened the bedroom door.

'Latifa! What's happened?'

'The exorcism went haywire! The jinnee is back inside Madame Gallisot.'

'What!'

'I went to wake her up. I'm choosey about who I do late breakfasts for. There was no reply so I decided to go in and give her a shake. But she'd been abducted by the jinnee.'

Ramzi ran to the room. The bed had been slept in, but the bathroom was cleared of toiletries and her wash bag and luggage gone.

He considered the possibilities. Either she had taken a plane back to Paris, or gone elsewhere. And elsewhere he reckoned to be the Blue Rocks at

Tafraoute. He hurried downstairs to the office, entered the combination of the safe and discovered Nicole's passport still inside.

Ramzi found her business card, and dialled the mobile number. Dead. He grabbed his keys and made his way through the medina lanes. Outside the ramparts people hovered or milled around with cases and plastic sacks. Beside their *grand* taxis, drivers shouted destinations, Essaouira! Essaouira! Ouarzazate! Ouarzazate! Agadir! Agadir! Eventually Ramzi found a taxi set for Tafraoute. The old Mercedes took six passengers: four in the back seat, two in the front. The driver had three passengers, and waited for three more. No, he said, there was no French woman. And his taxi was the one that ploughed that route. However, a bus had left earlier.

Ramzi whipped along to the *Gare Routière*, and found the appropriate ticket booth, number 21, half-hidden in shadows in the back. The man stopped counting dirhams into a cashbox and looked up. Yes, the bus had gone, and yes, he recalled a French woman, young with blond hair.

Ramzi reached for his mobile, but had forgotten it. Cursing, he returned to the riad. In the office, he phoned Abdelsaddek, but found him halfway to Essaouira with a carload of Dutch tourists. He phoned a second taxi driver, and a third, but no luck.

That put Ramzi at the mercy of madcap Kasim.

He realized he'd have to get a *grand* taxi. Slipping the two passports into a pocket he headed to his room, throwing a toothbrush and razor, clean underwear, a shirt, socks and sweater into a pile. On impulse, he added a pair of *Anasazi* climbing shoes on top, and carried it all downstairs. Various suitcases were locked in a cupboard by the entrance, but there was no time to search for the key. So instead of the Mulberry leather weekender he found a couple of ASWAK AS-SALAM supermarket bags in the kitchen, and pushed all the belongings into those.

'Keep her passport until she pays us!' Hisham yelled as Ramzi raced along the lane.

Panting he found the *grand* taxi to Tafraoute had left. Resigned to his fate, Ramzi rang Kasim.

'I'll be there in ten minutes, *inshallah*!'

God was willing, and the Mercedes screeched to a halt in five. The roof was dented—had it rolled over? Wincing at the broken taillight, Ramzi untied the cord that held the trunk shut, put his plastic bags inside and, dead man walking, climbed into the front seat. Kasim grinned, and lurched off.

Soon the pink walls of the city disappeared and they were hissing along the road, past the tangled hedges of Barbary Fig, past groves of olive trees, past a tractor and past roadside shacks selling pottery.

What a journey: overtaking on blind corners, potential head-on collisions, beeping of horns and klaxons, the yelp of tyres, and they had yet to reach the torturous Atlas road. Ramzi braced himself against each near miss until the armrest came off in his hand, much to Kasim's annoyance. Climbing the foothills, Kasim steered an erratic course, one hand on the wheel and his head craning out of the window to see the corners ahead, shifting between steep heart pulling hauls and sudden sprints. Misjudging a hairpin bend they slithered towards a precipice. The taxi spun as Kasim pulled the wheel hard right, foot hard on the brake—when Ramzi dared to open his eyes he saw they faced downhill rather than up. A three-point turn stalled as a minibus hurtled towards them with fairground screams, but unfazed, Kasim shot by at the last second. On the radio, a recitation of the Qur'an began. As they thundered onwards and upwards, Kasim turned the volume up full. Verse after verse rocked the car until Ramzi began to grasp the truth about the trip to the Blue Rocks. By then they were over the Tizi'n'test, and as the taxi rocketed down, Ramzi pushed back in his seat ready to hit g-force—

TWENTY-EIGHT

The hills and rocks that heralded Tafraoute seemed stained by the sunset. Passing a sign to the local hospital, the taxi skidded as Kasim slammed on the brakes.

'I'll drop you here. I have to be back at Marrakech to make an airport pick up at midnight—'

Ramzi paid and collected his bags of clothes. Kasim vanished in a cloud of exhaust fumes and dust. On shaky legs, Ramzi set off towards the town.

'Camels, donkeys, mountain bikes—'

Adjusting a Tuareg turban, a man hovered outside a shop, La Caverne des Nomades. It occurred to him that Nicole might already be cycling off to the Blue Rocks, so he stopped.

'I'm looking for a Frenchwoman. Young, attractive, blonde—'

'Not at this shop, Monsieur. But come inside and see my desert roses. Through here. Look at this one—'

'She's a friend. She might have rented a mountain bike?'

'No, not today.'

'I don't believe it!'

'Now you're calling me a liar?'

'No. The signed photograph on the wall. You're standing outside the shop with Chris Bonington. He's a climbing legend.'

'Yes, Monsieur Chris. He went up Everest, the southwest face, the hard way. He and his friends stayed here for two weeks. He told me the Anti-Atlas is the place he likes best to rock-climb.'

Ramzi lingered a few minutes in conversation, partially out of interest that the shopkeeper met one of his idols, and partially to delay an encounter with Nicole.

'Can you recommend a good hotel?'

'The Hotel Les Amandiers is just up the road. Most tourists go there. I can run you up if you like?'

The receptionist at the hotel raised an eyebrow at Ramzi's dishevelled appearance. As he handed over the key to a room, he heard a voice behind him.

'I like the designer luggage. Are you stalking me?'

'I brought your passport.'

'What service! Perhaps I can buy a drink to thank you? Say in half an hour?'

In his room, Ramzi pulled the crumpled clothes from the bag, trying to smooth out the creases. He had a long shower, and as he dressed, stared out to a vista of strange rock formations looming against the dusk. He knew what to say to Nicole, but returned downstairs as if he faced an execution. Still, if he'd survived the journey with Kasim, he could survive anything.

At a table outside, they ordered a bottle of *Gérouane Gris* wine. The heat of the day rose from the terrace. Over the desert, stars tumbled into the sky.

'It was a night like this, Ramzi. After the miscarriage, I felt depressed. I needed to be alone and walked off. Paul and Tahar called my name, but I pretended not to hear them. Well, you're a scientist Ramzi, so you'll smile at what I'm going to say next.'

'No, go on.'

'You see, I lay on the sand staring at the heavens. Soon I understood why stars made me long to weep: they were the souls of doomed children. So, the brightest of all should be the newest; it must be my baby, Walid.

'Then I thought, if the stars were the souls of infants, it would explain the endless lights of the universe, it would account for the firmament expanding. But I realized, in line with this law, the brightest star would edge away and fade as another replaced it. It would go on until it reached the end of the universe, and in time my baby would be lost from me.'

'It's certainly a hypothesis.'

'But the idea seemed so terrible. I ran through the night and when I'd run enough I threw back my head to scream and something strange happened. My howl seemed to gather me up, pulling me from the earth. For a few seconds, I had the impression I'd been levitated. At the same time, I sensed I was about to witness something, something in the darkness, something not fit for a human being to see.'

'Paul's colleague Bob Spasoff had a similar experience there.'

'Did he tell Tahar?'

'No, he told Paul.'

'Paul!'

A silence curdled between them. Ramzi poured more wine.

'What happened to Tahar after all of this?'

'What do you mean? He was with Paul at the campsite.'

'When did Tahar disappear?'

'I'd had a miscarriage. I took the first flight to Paris after we got back to Marrakech. Paul and I separated. It never crossed my mind check on Tahar.'

'Another thing: why did you act so strangely when we met the concierge Abdul Majid at Djemma el-Fna?'

'I was tired and emotional. Abdul Majid was always at me for tips.'

'Fine. But can you tell me this: who was the father of your child? Of Walid?'

'I beg your pardon?'

'I remembered at the cemetery after your husband's funeral you said, "Paul and I, we never had a child." When I thought it over it implied you had a child but with someone else other than Paul.'

'Semantics,' Nicole said, with visible relief.

'Nicole, in Marrakech you told Dr Rashida that you called your baby an Arabic name. You said you recited the Exordium from the Qur'an at his grave. If he had been Paul's child would you have done that?'

Nicole gulped some wine and refilled the

glass. Her hand trembled. She began to speak, differently from before.

'After all that business of string pulling, Paul finding a job, and my father's liver cancer, I flew to Marrakech. But from the moment I met Paul at the airport he appeared distracted, even distant. I put it down to the weeks we spent apart. I arrived and domestic life began.'

'How did you meet Tahar?'

'Paul brought him back from work for lunch. He hadn't told me, but I set a third place at the table, managing to eke out the charcuterie and salad. Conversation went OK, and I played the perfect hostess. But my smile was like a mask. I knew something was wrong and I should've seen it then.'

'What do you mean?' Ramzi said.

Nicole fiddled with the Tuareg amulet round her neck. 'As Paul talked to Tahar, he drifted into the patois of French Algeria.'

'When Paul stayed at the riad he did the same. It upset Hisham. He thought he was making fun of his French.'

'I can imagine. I considered mentioning it, but Paul persuaded Tahar to try out my Arabic. As if I wasn't embarrassed enough, Tahar spoke to me like a tiny child, asking my name.

'I said, "My name is Nour."'

'Nour?' Ramzi interrupted. 'As in, to shine and illuminate?'

'Yes. Well, Tahar's manner changed. He asked who had called me that. I explained about my North African friends in Clichy-sous-Bois. He started talking about when he studied in Paris. We talked and talked as if our lives depended on it until Paul interrupted in French. But Arabic was already spoken between us like a secret language.

'In the following days, I found my thoughts jumping back to Tahar, but put it down to my isolated existence. I tried to make the apartment more like a home. At first, I'd loved the spaciousness of the apartment and the exotic views over the Majorelle Gardens. But I started to hate the way the floor tiles threw echoes, maybe because I realized the hollowness was the sound of my relationship with Paul.

'Then one afternoon Paul returned from work and handed me a book of short stories by the Egyptian author, Mahmud Taimur.

'I said, "What's this?"

'Paul said, "It's a present from Tahar. He

thought you'd like something to read in Arabic."

'I hadn't seen a book, but a wedge. I passed it back to Paul. 'I said, "Tell him I've read it." Before Paul could protest, I walked away. But already a crack had opened between us.

'When Paul came home I asked about the ins and outs of his day at Ingémaroc. The one subject I never spoke of was Tahar. Thinking back, Paul probably sensed this, as he also treated the subject as taboo.

'Then it happened again. Another present from Tahar. A book of poetry. Stuck on the cover was a pink Post-it with the message, "Have you read this?" I pulled it off and underneath was the Arabic title of the slim volume. "The Ghost in her Veins." By Tahar Sediki.

'It was a signed edition, inscribed in beautiful handwritten Arabic: "To Nour." No, no mistake: the author was Tahar. The truth of it sent me spinning. I slapped the cover shut. Paul persuaded me not to send it back in case it upset Tahar. I quizzed him about the book; he had no idea who the writer was. And when I agreed to accept it, Paul kissed me lightly on the forehead. Later I thought of that kiss as a kiss of consent.

'What was Tahar like?'

'Sensitive. Entertaining. He loved his mother, and often spoke about her. How, for instance, she pronounced TV to be the instrument of Satan, so he bought her one. That was Tahar; his actions always took the measure of a person. And just as he watched his mother succumb to television's power, he must have watched as I succumbed to his.'

'You began to see each other alone?'

'One weekend Tahar arranged a picnic at Lalla Takerkoust. You know, the lake with the dam not far from Marrakech. But the night before Héloïse phoned from Nice with the news that Paul's father had a heart attack. He'd been playing a game of boules. He made one of those high lobs he kept boasting about and collapsed. Hearing this, I almost laughed. Héloïse painted a dramatic picture of him lying in a spaghetti of tubes and wires in intensive care. Paul wanted us both to dash to his bedside. But on the next plane to Marseilles, the only seats left were extortionate. We agreed it better if I stayed.

'As I drove Paul to the airport, we remembered the picnic. I wanted to cancel but Paul said I'd be silly not to go. He telephoned Tahar. From the jist of the call, he was reluctant, but Paul insisted,

214

making it hard for either of us to object.

'So Tahar and I had the picnic *à deux*. We hardly spoke during the journey and at one stage I almost asked him to turn back. Soon we circled the dam, and in some way the lunar landscape made me feel I lived on another planet. We found a secluded cove, parked and went down to the water's edge and spread a kilim under a tamarisk tree. I arranged the food. Afterwards we went for a swim, and as we lay on the kilim to dry, I confess I was the one who made the first move. Unable to control myself, I slid my fingers under the waistband of his swimsuit. And then he kissed me. He was delicate, so delicate, but I felt shattered into a thousand pieces.'

'And afterwards?'

'We started meeting. It was not easy. Even in Marrakech, it's difficult for a Moroccan and a European to rent a hotel room together. Tahar had an apartment in Guéliz. To begin with we made love there.

'Well, do you know something Ramzi? Surrender and love leaves you vulnerable. To protect myself, I became very watchful of Paul. Of course, I didn't know then what I know now, and I misinterpreted things.'

'Such as?'

'I noticed Paul looked at Tahar in puzzling ways. Sometimes his eyes filled with a desperate desire I saw as a longing to know the truth. Sometimes I saw the way Paul checked out Tahar's body, and I only thought he imagined the two of us making love in bed. At the same time, Paul's manner became remote. As for sex, he was never in the mood. Knowing the little I did, what could I conclude? This was Paul's way to let me know he'd tumbled to my affair with Tahar? That he was waiting for me to come to my senses? Of course, in hindsight, I can see Paul was either infatuated or falling in love with Tahar.'

'But you and Tahar still saw each other?'

'Yes of course. He even began to come to our apartment when Paul was at work.'

'But what about the other woman he was seen with?'

'The other woman! What other woman?'

'Muslim. She wore a burqa, gloves, the whole shebang.'

Nicole gave a peal of laughter. How lovely she looked!

'What's so funny?'

'Because I was the woman!'

'What? You're kidding?'

'You seem shocked. But it let me go around Marrakech with Tahar incognito. Covering myself with the burqa, it felt like a game. I had to find a new way of walking. It took some time before I stopped miscalculating distances. I'd leave the apartment dressed like that to meet him, and together we'd walk the streets of Marrakech without a care in the world. It was thrilling if we met someone we knew.'

'Did the concierge Abdul Majid put two and two together, and start blackmailing you?'

'He'd known for a while. I remember the day, so beautiful from the balcony, the blue sky, the warm sun, the palms, the snowy Atlas, and as Tahar put his arm around me, we watched a white egret fly by. Life seemed so perfect. Then Paul phoned. He was supposed to be out of town, but something had cropped up and he'd be home in half an hour. Tahar got dressed and ran. The front door clicked. I turned on the shower, but the doorbell went. I thought Tahar had forgotten something. Pulling on a dressing gown, I ran to answer. However, the shadow on the landing was wrong: too short, too skinny. And instead of Tahar I found myself face to face with Abdul Majid.

'He said, "I want two-thousand dirhams."'

'I played it cool. I told him that Paul dealt with the condominium bills. But Abul Majid repeated the demand. Two thousand dirhams. And if I didn't pay up then and there he'd tell Paul that Tahar visited the apartment after he went off to work.

'I laughed and explained Tahar was just a friend. Abdul Majid smiled, and pulled out a piece of paper and began reading a list of dates and arrival and departure times.

'I had little option but to pay him. From the sideboard drawer, I grabbed a handful of dirhams, glad for once about Paul's carelessness with cash. Do you know what Abdul Majid did? He licked his thumb, and insisted on counting out the notes in front of me. The humiliation of it made the blood hammer in my ears. When he left I fell to my knees, sobbing. But knowing Paul was due home, I managed to crawl to the shower, and when he came through the door everything appeared normal.'

'But what did you do after that? Did you keep paying up?'

'Abdul Majid's blackmail was a reality check. Did Paul suspect? If he chose to say nothing, it demonstrated the underlying strength of our marriage, and I was reluctant to jeopardize it even more. If he said nothing, it showed the strength of his love. And at the same time, I realized that to save Tahar, I had to end the affair as soon as possible.

'Next day, Paul cast the die. When he came home from work he announced he'd invited Tahar to dinner that evening. After an eternity, Tahar bounced in, surprising us with a gift of three artichokes. He said they were aphrodisiacs.

'Paul went bright red—I remember that. He took Tahar to the kitchen to prepare them. I laid cutlery for three. My hands were shaking. I had to escape, so I disappeared to the spare bedroom to fold laundry.

'Soon the artichokes were ready, and Paul called me to the table. I felt like I was walking off the edge of a cliff. I still recall every detail. The beautiful objects were on the table at our places. As we sat down, the chair legs scraped on the tiles. We started the meal; leaf after leaf was torn away and dipped in melted butter, and one by one, the chewed leaves were discarded into a bowl as the artichokes were reduced to nothing. The ritual killed me by inches. Finally, Paul and Tahar's plates were mopped clean, but I had no appetite to take the fibrous choke from the top of the heart left on my plate.

'At this point Paul's father phoned. Summoning all my courage I told Tahar in Arabic I no longer wished to see him. I had tried to foresee his reaction, but nothing was as hurtful as the reality: no storm crossed his face, nor did it look vengeful or distressed. He wiped the butter from his fingers with a napkin, and without a single word to me, said *bonsoir* to Paul, and left.'

'Bob told me that Tahar was moody and jumpy in the weeks before your trip.'

'He did? He said that? Please don't tell me that!'

Nicole jumped up, rocking the table. Ramzi grabbed the wine bottle as a glass fell over. As she rushed from the terrace, he wondered if she'd come back. The desert night grew chilly. He walked into the hotel, but found Nicole, crouched down and examining some geraniums in the small interior patio.

'Are you OK?'

She stood up. 'I hadn't realized—'

'The breakup might have hurt Tahar?'

'Let's have dinner.'

Neither felt hungry, and opted to share a tagine. Ramzi ordered a bottle of red wine.

'How did you feel after the split?'

'Relief. To be honest, I even considered myself a paragon of virtue. I began to dominate, telling Paul to take me here and there. I started making a nest, and dreamed how happy we would be.'

'But you were still being blackmailed?'

'He came for money once. But I asked Paul for the jeep, to go shopping at Marjane, the hypermarket. When I reached home, Abdul Majid was sitting across from the entrance. I drove the jeep at high speed in his direction, braking at the last minute. He screamed and fell off his chair. But he got the message.'

'And then?'

'And then I felt an ache. At first, it was barely perceptible, but it started to consume me. I'd take the veil, crushing it against my face, leaving it wet with tears. Tahar's book of poetry became irresistible. I read and reread the pages until I almost knew them by heart.

'One afternoon, I heard Paul at the door, and snapped the book shut. He broke the news that Tahar had suggested a weekend away at the Blue Rocks. What game was Tahar playing, suggesting a weekend away, the three of us together? The fact he refused to respect my wishes made my blood boil. Now this proposal of a trip, I thought it utter madness.

'I remember saying, "Why can't we go, just the two of us together?" Believe me Ramzi, at that moment, in all honesty, I longed for nothing more.'

Nicole shivered. The tagine arrived. By tacit agreement, for the rest of the evening, they made no mention of Paul and Tahar.

THIRTY

Nervous about what the day might bring, Ramzi found Nicole's high spirits at breakfast difficult to reconcile with the revelations of the night before.

'I like the kinky shoes,' Nicole said.

Ramzi laughed. 'They have a fetish for rocks.'

Leaving the hotel they bought bottled water and hired mountain bikes at La Caverne des Nomades. The owner offered to put directions to the Blue Rocks down on paper and uncapped a fountain pen.

'Look at this crystal. It's like a flower.'

'Yes *madame*, it's called a desert rose.'

Nicole bought it. Directions in hand they left the shop, and sped along tarmac into a wilderness dotted with boulders and stacked rocks. As instructed, after a short cycle south, they took their bearings from a startling colossus nicknamed Napolean's Hat.

Twenty minutes later, they arrived at Jean Vérame's Blue Rocks. With the paint worn and fading, perhaps the impact was not as impressive as twenty years ago. Nonetheless, against the strange, otherworldly landscape, the effect still was mesmerizing. Ramzi understood why the artist needed the help of the fire brigade—some boulders stood as high as a house, and even to a rock climber, looked daunting.

Ramzi narrowed his eyes against the sun, taking in the rocks and scrub and the horizon of hills, but the remoteness of the place and the eerie silence laid a chill hand across him. He understood the fear in Bob's voice as he'd told his story and why Nicole's face looked so troubled.

They started off across the parched landscape. The bikes made it hard, hot work. Eventually they spotted a solitary rock ahead, tall and slightly curved on one side, much like a robed figure. Dismounting, they walked with the bikes towards it.

Ramzi expected to stop there, but Nicole pushed on towards a daunting boulder split in two. Her pace slowed, she abandoned the bike, and Ramzi saw it up ahead.

Against the landscape the cairn looked

insignificant. Nicole knelt in front of the small cone that marked her baby's grave. Ramzi stood a few steps away, as she unwrapped the desert rose and fitted it into the pile of rocks. After some time, he laid a hand on her shoulder.

'Nicole. Let's get out of the sun.'

She nodded. He helped her up, towards the shade cast by the boulder. Wary of snakes and scorpions, they sat down on the sand. Ramzi twisted the cap off a bottle, and shared the tepid water. After a few moments, he summoned the courage to speak.

'How are you feeling? Are you thinking about that night?'

'Over and over. At first, the fact no one had known I'd lost the baby made me happy. It was dusk, and it wrapped around me, protected me. I carried on as normal. By the light of the Campingaz lantern I opened plastic boxes of cold chicken and a salad and added a dressing. Meanwhile Tahar boiled some water on the stove, added it to a bowl of couscous and fluffed the grains with a fork. Paul opened a bottle of wine. Tahar declined, but the red wine went straight to my head. I stumbled and fell flat on my face, but laughed as Paul pulled me up.

'To my astonishment, Tahar made a comment

about how he hated women who got drunk. When I heard that, something snapped. I threw the contents of my cup over his white T-shirt, and told him I hated Muslims who stank of booze.

'He stood up. I remember his head and hands were shaking, as if he were about to fly off the ground. "She's crazy," Tahar said. "I don't understand any of this."

'He walked away, and after a few metres, stopped and threw his head back as if struggling for breath. Then he tore off his T-shirt, threw it into the dust and crouched down to unzip the tent and crawled in to change.

'My mind reeled. This was a side of Tahar I hadn't seen. When he returned, Paul acted as peacemaker. But later, as we ate supper, I'd made some comment about the soulless suburbs mushrooming around Marrakech. "So, what did you expect to find?" Tahar asked. "A city from the Arabian Nights? I can just see it: gold dust on the streets, jewel-studded palaces, and pearl covered chariots!'

'My blood froze. And then, out of the blue, Paul produced a box of fireworks. He lit a firecracker, and lobbed it into the distance. I found it terrifying. It sounded like gunshots ricocheting between the rocks and boulders.

'I couldn't stand it, and clasped my hands to my ears. But Tahar cheered and applauded. Paul ripped open a paper packet, handing out sparklers. We lit them one by one, and scribbled them against the darkness. Tahar's sparkler was the last. But as we watched it move from right to left, Paul said, "That looks like Arabic."

'Tahar said, "Yes, it was the word, *nour*. It means light."

'That's what me mad and the moment I ran off into the desert.'

'Did you tell them about it?'

'When I got back to the camp, Paul treated me like a naughty teenager who had stayed out past her curfew. He thought he'd heard a scream, but I changed the subject. I wondered where Tahar was and if he'd gone out looking for me. But according to Paul, he was already in his tent, sleeping. What a fool I felt when I heard that!

'I woke early but found myself alone. I'd slept in my clothes, so crawled out of the tent. But what I saw shocked me. Paul stood beside Tahar, and held his hand in his.

'I said, "Oh, what a touching scene." Paul started on about Tahar's hand looking infected. Tahar told him to stop fussing. I remember he said, "I'm not going to die. In fact, after breakfast, I'm going to climb that boulder."

'Paul said he'd join him. I told them I'd go too. I still don't understand it. After miscarrying my baby, I should have been exhausted, but something, some force revitalized me.

'But first Tahar boiled water to make coffee. I'd brought crêpes and fresh orange juice from Marrakech. But I don't think anyone had any appetite. I sensed we all had a fixation with climbing the boulder. And after all that happened, I began to believe a jinnee had possessed us.'

She paused. A minute passed before she continued. 'When I see it now, I wonder how we ever reached the top. But we did. And that's where it happened.'

'Go on.'

'You see this crack just beside us? It opens up on top. There's a cleft and to reach the highest point, we had to cross it. Paul bounded across and I followed. Tahar came last. But he miscalculated the jump and fell into the crevice.'

THIRTY-ONE

'I'm not going to die. That's what he said. I'll never forget that's what he said.'

Ramzi stood up and stepped back a few paces to judge the boulder. Some of it looked as steep as the climbs he'd made in the Alps. He knew from experience boulder climbing took extraordinary energy and stamina—more suited to the sprinter— whilst rock climbing was more dependent on endurance. As a result, the first thing Ramzi thought was: Paul, Nicole, Tahar, they were insane. It seemed a miracle they had reached the top at all. But he remembered Zahra's story about Tahar spending his school holidays helping tourists clamber up the rocks to the highest cataracts in the Ourika Valley. 'The Goat Boy'.

Ramzi felt compelled to climb the rock himself. Nicole clutched his arm. 'Ramzi, don't go.

You'll get hurt.'

He shook her off.

After determining the best ascent, Ramzi started to scramble up. He found the boulder featureless, but the surface not dissimilar to 'God's own rock', English millstone grit, which provided some friction. But as he climbed there were fewer crimpy handholds and he was convinced his feet would slip. Panting, he hauled himself over and onto the top. He tugged at his polo shirt, to stop the perspiration sticking it to his skin. Nicole stood below, lost in the landscape.

What dark power had brought the three of them, two with no climbing experience, safely to this point? The top of the boulder sloped upwards from where Ramzi stood, but on the surface, the fracture had widened to form a crevice. As Nicole has said, to reach the highest part this had to be crossed.

Walking over, he crouched beside it. The abyss was about a metre wide, but narrowed at each end. The sun blazed overhead, but failed to penetrate the depths of the chasm. Ramzi picked up a chunk of stone flaked from the surface and dropped it. Yet no thud broke the absolute silence of the void.

Ramzi stepped back, took a short run, and

leapt across. Easy, yes; though not without risk. But it confirmed his doubts.

Having come this far he decided to descend into the crevice. Ramzi edged in, his back against one side of rock. Glad for having worn the Anasazi shoes, he placed a foot on the wall in front at about knee height, and positioned the other foot against the wall behind. With hands on opposite walls, palms against the rock, he pushed down with his legs and arms at the same time until his was fully extended, then switched feet and shifted his hands. Gradually, he inched downwards towards its depths.

After a time, he paused and stared up at the ribbon of blue sky. The clairvoyance of Lalla Meriyum, the *shuwafa* hired by Tahar's mother, was remarkable. The alleyway with the high walls was this crevice. Ramzi might have laughed, but for the fact it reinforced the notion that Tahar's body laid at the bottom.

The way the chasm narrowed at each end of the boulder made it impossible for any man to escape through. The only way out was up. If Tahar had fallen in, plunging to this depth, and had not died on impact, it would be a safe bet he'd break one or both legs, or even an arm. Even if Tahar knew how to climb a rock chimney, as Ramzi climbed now, it would be impossible with shattered limbs.

Ramzi continued, shifting left to avoid a rock jammed between the walls of the chasm. Something soft and springy touched his hand. Heart thumping, he realized the object was made of some type of textile. In the end, he stretched his hand across it. The material gave way to the hard visor of a baseball cap. Ramzi grabbed it and in the gloom managed to make out the white logo embroidered on the front. He had seen one before, in Bob Spasoff's 4x4.

Ingémaroc.

For safekeeping, he pulled the cap on his head and descended faster, keeping pressure in his legs and knees, and his back against the rock. But after another two or three metres he felt nervous. He had come down maybe five metres, which he guessed might have been the height of the boulder. Yet below there was no sign of the bottom of the crevice, just darkness.

For a moment Ramzi had an overpowering desire to relax, to release the tension between his body and the rock. He knew if he did, that he'd fall to meet the same fate as Tahar. How very easy it would be to surrender to the shadows below—

'Ramzi?'

The distant voice, Nicole's, tugged him out of his reverie. Summoning all his courage and strength he started to work his way up towards the light. Finally, Ramzi climbed out onto the surface, and lay breathless in the heat.

Recovered, he sat up, examining the green baseball cap. Inside were two initials marked in black pen, T.S. And in the hard sunlight, Ramzi saw what looked like a spatter of blood.

'Ramzi?'

He stood up. 'I'm OK. I'm coming down.'

That said he didn't start at once. He tried to imagine how Tahar fell. He must have knocked his head on the rock on the chasm, dislodging the baseball cap as he dropped further. Ramzi folded the hat flat, stuffed it into a trouser pocket, and mustering the last reserves of energy, negotiated the way down the side of the boulder.

The concentration cleared his mind. All at once, he knew what had happened.

THIRTY-TWO

Back on terra firma, Nicole handed over a bottle of water, which he gulped down.

'What were you up to?' Nicole said, brushing the back of his shirt. 'All these marks and look, you've ripped it here.'

Without saying a word, Ramzi put his hand in his pocket, and pulled out the Ingémaroc baseball cap. Nicole paled. Turning it over, she walked away. After a few steps, she crumpled to the ground. Ramzi knelt at her side.

'There's blood. There's blood,' she wept. 'He must have hit his head. Why don't you tell me how he fell?'

At first, she didn't appear to understand, and wiped her eyes.

'I told you.'

'Nicole, Tahar used to spend his summers as a tourist guide, scrambling up the rocks at the cascades in the Ourika Valley. I doubt he could have misjudged that jump.'

With a look of exhaustion, she said, 'I told Paul about Tahar, about us, about the affair. He had a fit. We both know why: Paul was gay. He loved Tahar too, in every sense. I think Paul lived a fantasy where his feelings would be reciprocated, and they'd walk into the sunset together. He lashed out and Tahar stumbled back, and slipped into the crevice.

'I wanted to protect Paul. After the pathetic incident with the rent-boy, and now that he's dead, it doesn't seem necessary anymore. Tragedy, it's a pattern in his family. Paul blamed himself. That's why I think he went back to Marrakech. He was trying to find Tahar's mother. To make an act of contrition.'

'I'm sorry Nicole. First you told me Tahar fell to his death by accident. And now Paul pushed him because he found out about your affair.'

'You can believe whatever you want. Take your pick.'

'I'll tell you what I believe. I believe Tahar was pushed, not by Paul, but by you, Nicole.'

'How can you say that? I loved him!'

'Strange to say, the day Paul died, I bought a book on murders in North London. Let me tell you about Ruth Ellis. She was the last woman to be hanged in Britain. She shot her lover, killed him with four bullets. It had all the marks of a crime of passion, except in Britain a crime of passion is no defence. You see, Ruth Ellis had been pregnant, and her lover punched her in the stomach and triggered a miscarriage a few days before. Fifty years have gone by, and the family is still challenging her conviction. They claim the extreme emotional and psychological impact of miscarriage caused her to kill her lover. Listen Nicole, I think something similar happened to you.'

Ramzi wondered if he'd gone too far. Nicole trembled, but to his relief, didn't cry, or relapse into some hideous state.

'Ramzi, believe me. Time after time I weighed what happened until my mind blocked it out. Believe me, I was not the person who pushed him. When I saw myself at the Blue Rocks I saw another person.

'The night I lost my baby, after I returned to the campsite, Paul turned in, but I stayed up alone. I felt betrayed, betrayed by Tahar.

'There was no way round it. I became

convinced that because of Tahar, I had lost our little one. Weighing this up, something inside me took over.'

'Paul climbed up the face of the boulder first. I went next and Tahar came behind. The ascent wasn't easy and I could hear my heart hammering.

'But at the top, as you saw, we had to make that small jump. Paul leapt first. I was nervous but Paul held out his hand and I made it across. Once I was on my feet Paul walked a few steps on. Tahar jumped behind me, but landed precariously close to the edge. He reached out to steady himself.

'I stretched out my arm. Tahar raised his hand to clasp mine. Our eyes met and Tahar smiled his beautiful smile. I gripped his injured knuckles and squeezed hard. He winced and tried to free his hand and that unbalanced him. I let go: maybe I gave a small push, I'm still not sure. All I know is that he stepped back and slid down into the abyss.

'Paul hadn't seen what happened, and wouldn't have understood it if he did. He heard the noise. He turned. "Where's Tahar?" he said. He sounded like a lost boy.

'I said he'd slipped. Paul lay face down on the rock and howled Tahar's name into the chasm, but we heard no answer. We waited an hour, maybe two, in case he'd been knocked unconscious, and came round, but at the end of it, still no reply.'

'You left him there. I suppose you weren't thinking and Paul—'

'No. Paul wanted to raise the alarm in Tafraoute and rescue Tahar. But I persuaded him that we risked putting our lives in jeopardy. I took control, not Paul.

'We managed to climb back down the boulder. I told Paul that when we got back to Marrakech, to say that Tahar pulled out and I'd been ill, so in the end we decided not to have gone on the trip. To back up the story, I'd leave for Paris on the first plane. Of course, that suited me.

'We rushed around and dismantled the campsite. Afterwards we drove back in silence. Paul had to pull over a couple of times, because he was crying so hard. In the end, I took the wheel.

'Then we had a piece of luck. On the radio, we heard about the bombings in Casablanca, and how the police were scouring the country for the terrorists behind it. Because of that I knew we were in the clear. If the company reported Tahar's disappearance, the police would link him to the bombings, and imagine he'd gone into hiding or on the run.'

'That's what happened—'

She smiled. 'It was almost too easy. All we had to do was hold our nerve, keep our heads down and cover our tracks. Arriving back in Marrakech resembled the end of a wild dream. We went directly to a street market outside the ramparts, near your riad in fact, and gave them Tahar's clothes and bag to sell, no questions asked. Back home, Paul started sorting out the jeep, and I went up to the apartment. And—' Her expression changed.

'Did something happen?'

'An envelope. I found an envelope lying on the floor in the hall. Addressed in Arabic. To Nour.'

'A letter?' Ramzi said. 'From Tahar?'

'At first I thought I'd gone crazy. That Tahar had somehow survived and beaten us to Marrakech. But I remembered the forgotten backpack. He'd staged it to leave the letter.'

'May I ask, what did it say?'

'It's here.' Nicole took the Tuareg amulet from around her neck and unfastened it. Folded inside were two sheets of airmail paper, exquisitely handwritten in Arabic script. She handed them to Ramzi.

My beloved,

It has now been several days perhaps a century since I last saw you. This is a difficult letter to write, but I am writing it now as later I may not have the strength to do so. Before we met, your husband—I must call him this to drum your union into my mind—told me you spoke Arabic. I confess I was skeptical, and when I was invited for that first lunch at your apartment I expected you to spend the afternoon looking for a chance to mention some phrase like 'Ali took the camel to the market.' But from the moment I heard your Arabic, your flawless Arabic, my blood quickened at hearing the word of God on your lips. That was the beginning; it should have been the end. Nour, you disassembled me, and recreated a man whose whole being threatened to fly heavenward, who heard only the language of his own beating heart. Our love our discordant love. For how else can I describe it if I consider the schisms between us? I am Moroccan; you are French. I am Muslim; you are Christian. I am single and you are married.

It seems our love was nothing more than a game. I shouldn't be surprised as Morocco is the perfect place to play games. Mysteries are impenetrable, rites are obscure, and in Marrakech, where the sun burns from a blue sky more often than not, the days come and go without touching us, forcing people to create their own tempests.

I became used to games in France. Thinking I was equal until in the street or in the métro I became the victim of a racist slur. But no words were as wounding as when you told me it was over. I left in silence, because if I'd opened my mouth to protest, a scream would have cut loose, for in that instant I was falling from the top of a minaret to the bottom of a well. In the dark days that followed I tried to adjust, but my reactions were erratic. At times, I was possessed by an emptiness so unimaginable I thought I might break from the world; at other times, I was consumed by a rage that made me want to raise my fists at the heavens, at providence, at God.

I stumbled on. Outside, silk and embroideries, but within, a scorpion of anguish dwelt in a sorely stricken heart. Then my wildest desires were answered. Your husband came to me to arrange a weekend away. Of course, immediately I said no. But when he told me you had insisted I go with you, my hopes soared.

I toyed with the practicalities of the future, a future together. You would divorce and we would marry. For, as you know, I dream of starting my own engineering office. In my mind, I saw you here in Marrakech, together in a new home, putting your arm around me, and telling me it had been a splendid day.

These sparks lit a firebrand, which I whirled into a long line of fire. But by degrees the flames faded, and I became prey to bitter thoughts. Unavoidably I brooded over your husband. I value him as a true friend, someone I can trust to help me if ever I was in difficulty. Yet, knowing this, I betrayed him, monstrously so. I thought of him, of you, of myself, and concluded our adultery was wrong, and completely reckless.

I don't know what will happen to this letter. I'll go to Tafraoute and the Blue Rocks. But if I have the courage, before we go I'll slide this letter under your door, to let you see these inadequate words, and to help you understand why we cannot see each other again when we return.

Or maybe one day, I'll tell you—it's because of you I'm alive.

Tahar'

Nicole broke the silence.

'The fact Paul told me that Tahar arranged the trip changed everything. If I'd known, Tahar and our baby might be alive today. Instead Paul's dead. Tahar's dead. And our baby's dead.'

THIRTY-THREE

Back at the La Caverne des Nomades, Nicole propped her bike against the wall and without a word strode off to the hotel.

'You need a drink,' the storeowner said to Ramzi.

'How do you know?'

'I've seen it before. Most tourists come, see the Blue Rocks, take a few snaps, and go on their way. But for the others, some hidden power, we call it a jinnee, affects them.' He unlocked a trunk and pulled out a bottle of *Glenmorangie* whisky and a glass.

The sight of it made Ramzi feel even more wretched, and his eyes became tearful.

'Why don't you warn people?'

'What would that do for tourism? I'd be hounded out of Tafraouate.'

Ramzi changed the subject.

'If you ever have a group of climbers, or Chris Bonington is here again, could you let me know?'

'Do you have a card?'

Ramzi took out his wallet, and handed over one of the new business cards for Riad Waqi. Moisture on his thumb smudged the photograph.

'Nice riad. I like the small map on the back. Monsieur, are you OK?'

Ramzi felt either blood or the whisky gallop to his head.

'Yes, let me just sit down for a minute.'

A tourist came into the shop, looking at the desert roses and a pile of Tuareg trinkets, distracting the shopkeeper. Ramzi's mind raced. The business card explained Paul's murder.

How had Tahar's mother found Riad Waqi? Ramzi made no mention of it, and in Setti Fatma he'd handed over the card that only showed his name and personal mobile number. No address. Yet she turned up at the riad after seeing Lalla Maryiam. He straightened the pattern of events in his mind.

Paul had taken the last couple of the riad's business cards. He visited Tahar's mother at home. The ten thousand euros in Paul's travel wallet was blood money, to atone. That meant he had confessed to what happened. But Zahra had been proud and principled enough to refuse it, even though she survived with the bleak reality that her son could no longer provide income. Without a body and death certificate she could not access any money she might inherit.

Paul left one of the business cards, in case she changed her mind. But what Zahra wanted was revenge.

Ramzi pictured the man skulking in the lane on the night Paul died. With the address, Paul's name and description, he followed him. And later, as Paul left the rent-boy, the man caught him alone, and cut his throat. As for the assailant's identity, it would, no doubt, remain unknown. Yet, in keeping with Inspector Karim's 'cliché', Tahar's mother came to Riad Waqi as it was connected to the crime, to see where Paul had stayed, to imagine his last moments, to perhaps give her a tremor of power.

'Another whisky?'

'No thanks. Can I offer to pay?'

'No, you needed it.'

He returned to the hotel, showered and changed his clothes. At the reception he asked a question, even though he knew the answer.

'Madame Gallisot? She checked out about ten minutes ago.'

THIRTY-FOUR

It was a relief to leave the eeriness of the Blue Rocks and the grip of malevolence surrounding them. But barely an hour went by without Ramzi wondering whether the power behind what happened had been a jinnee or as Dr Rashida put it, the subconscious, which in some monstrous way drove the three of them to end their relationship in tragedy. Ramzi returned from Tafraoute alone. As he expected, Nicole was not at the riad, and he hadn't heard from or contacted her since. He understood why Nicole acted as she did. But he couldn't forgive the pact of silence with Paul.

That said, he'd made himself an accomplice. Ramzi knew where Tahar's body lay, how he died, and who killed him. He considered contacting Inspector Karim, but whilst he had no problem explaining the discovery of the body in a crevice in the desert, it would implicate Nicole. For all his disappointment with her, verging on disgust, he did not want to do this. In the end, of course, nothing could be proved anyway.

What had he achieved? Science applied to the human condition? Ramzi took Paul's murder and Tahar's disappearance, constructed several hypotheses, and by eliminating them one by one reached a solution. But in science the solution would have a consequence, and in this case punishment for a crime. Nicole might suffer for her mistake, if her conscience allowed. Paul had attempted to atone, but Tahar's mother had demanded more than money.

About a week after he returned from the Blue Rocks, Ramzi asked Abdelsadak to drive him back to Setti Fatma. Ramzi climbed the steep lane to the blue front door and found Zahra sweeping the step. They exchanged greetings of peace.

'I've been waiting for you, sir.'

She ushered him in and performed the tea making ritual. Ramzi now noticed the television in the corner that Tahar had bought for his mother.

'You knew your son was dead,' he said.

'Lalla Meriyum is a very famous *shuwafa*.'

'No, I mean before that. Paul Gallisot came here, told you, and offered you money as an act of contrition.'

'It was blood money. I refused it.'

'Yes, but in case you changed your mind Paul left our business card. It's the only way you could have found out about Riad Waqi and the address.'

'I see.'

'You arranged for Paul to be murdered.'

Zahra finished her glass of tea.

'Tell me sir, what are your plans? To call the police and have me put in prison? Myonly son is dead. I will never have grandchildren. Sir, I am already in prison.'

Regret tinged Ramzi's feeling of repulsion. With nothing more to say, he returned to Marrakech. Nursing a glass of wine that evening in Riad Waqi, Ramzi recalled the word Nicole had used—tragedy. In the end Ramzi tried to draw a line under the matter, and decided to visit Paul's grave at the European cemetery.

The following morning, a bouquet of mixed roses in hand, Ramzi took a left onto the Rue Erraouda. A taxi waited outside the cemetery gate. He walked towards the white cenotaph, and turned along the avenue. An elderly man strolled in his direction, and greeted him in French. Ramzi returned the greeting; the man looked familiar, but he couldn't place him.

Here amongst the tombs and mausoleums Nicole's words still rang in his ears: 'Can you imagine being abandoned to that awful silence?' The thought of Tahar, forsaken at the Blue Rocks, would always prey on Ramzi's mind.

Reaching the grave, Ramzi saw the mound had subsided, and a headstone marked it: *Paul Gallisot 1977-2004*. The wreaths left by Héloïse and Nicole were weathered into wire skeletons. But beside them lay fresh flowers with a card.

Resting the roses next to them, Ramzi noticed droplets on the petals. A few weeds picked from the mound were thrown aside, but still looked alive. Crouching down, he read the card. On it was written an epitaph: *Né fils—Mort inconnu*.

Born a son, died a stranger. In that instant Ramzi realized the elderly man he'd passed minutes ago was Paul's father. Ramzi left the grave, running back towards the gate, but the elderly European had gone. Yet, what could he do? Try to track the man down to justify Paul and his actions?

Ramzi concluded the exercise was pointless. Instead he headed back to the medina. Inside the ramparts he passed the alleyway that led to the unfinished house presented by the Black Sultan to the holy saint. For a moment Ramzi hesitated until a scooter swerved to block his way.

'Haj Ali!'

In Arabic, they exchanged elaborate greetings. Satisfied, the *muqaddam* adjusted his fez.

'Well, Monsieur Ramzi, are your managing to keep your guests alive?'

'Against all odds. We had a murderess staying with us only last week.'

Unsure if the shriek was human or tyre-rubber, Ramzi waved away the cloud of exhaust fumes. At Riad Waqi a dejected Hisham stood polishing the brass plaque beside the front door.

'What's wrong?'

'We're sunk, Monsieur Ramzi.'

'Sunk?'

'Dr Rashida sent her bill.'

'How much?'

'It's sealed and addressed to you. Imagine, not only Dr Rashida's fees, but the charges for the Grand Master, the Arifa, the Gnawa musicians, the cost of the incense—'

Ramzi ripped open the envelope. On the headed-paper he read: 'Fee for medical services to

Riad Waqi: an invitation to dinner with Monsieur Ramzi.'

Ramzi blushed. Peering over his shoulder, Hisham perked up.

'Take her to the food stalls at Djemma el-Fna. We're a bit tight this month.'

Next in the Ramzi series—

SHADOWS OF ESSAOUIRA

Escaping drama at Riad Waqi and the heat of a
Marrakech summer, Ramzi travels to Essaouira on
the Atlantic, a secretive and windblown place,
adorned with mysterious signs and symbols. Checking
into a B&B he is intrigued to find the other guests are
Jewish, having arrived from overseas to prepare for
the annual Hiloula pilgrimage to venerate the
nineteenth century saint, *tzadik* Rabbi Haim Pinto.
Colliding with Dr Rashida, taking a break to windsurf,
his holiday seems perfect. But when one of the party
dies after a ceremonial feast, Ramzi cannot resist
investigating. Is it food poisoning or murder?
Joining forces, he and Dr Rashida uncover dark and
far-reaching tales of retribution and Essaouira's
former Jewish community.

GLOSSARY

Alhamdulilla—'Praise to God.'

Arifa—female assistant to the Grand Master in an exorcism.

Ashura—a festival that marks two historical events: the day Noah left the Ark, and the day that Moses was saved from the Egyptians by God.

Bab—old gateway in the city walls.

Baraka—a divine blessing.

Beur—a colloquial term to designate French-born people whose parents are immigrants from North Africa. The word was coined by reversing the syllables of the word *arabe* in French. For example, "arabe" became "a-ra-beu" then "beu-ra-a" and "beur" by contraction.

Bism'illah—'In the name of God.'

B'hou—part of a riad that resembles an alcove with seating.

Burqa—loose clock covering a woman from head to toe worn by some conservative Muslims in public.

Derb—lane in the medina.

Djemma el-Fna—the main square of the old city of Marrakech.

Djullanah the Sea-girl—from the story in the '1001 Arabian Nights.' Sea-people are human in form, but can breath underwater.

Douriya —a small apartment in the riad, traditionally used by the eldest son.

Eid al-Adha—Feast of the Sacrifice, an important religious holiday.

Fairuz—famous Lebanese female singer.

Fez—a close-fitting, flat-topped, brimless hat shaped like a truncated cone. It is red felt or cloth with a silk tassel and worn in Morocco as a symbol of nationalism.

Ginbri —traditional musical stringed instrument.

Gnawa—Black-African Islamic spiritual music. In Moroccan popular culture, *Gnawas*, through their ceremonies, are considered to be experts in the magical treatment of scorpion stings and psychic disorders. They play deeply low-toned hypnotic trance music and dance to evoke ancestral saints who can drive out evil.

Guéliz—the commercial part of the modern town built by the French in Marrakech during the

Protectorate.

Sidi Harazem—still bottled mineral water.

Harissa—hot chilli paste.

Hivernage—the residential quarter of the modern town built by the Franch in Marrakech during the Protectorate.

Hunja—spicy cinnamon tea.

Inshallah—'God Willing.'

Jellaba—a loose-fitting ankle-length hooded robe.

Khettaras—underground systems of irrigation that stretched for kilometers and enabled the planting of the city's palm groves and gardens besides supplying adequate water to the ancient medina.

Kilim—flat-weave rug.

La—'No.'

Medina—the historic walled city in Marrakech.

Mouna—a cake soaked with orange flower water to celebrate Easter in French colonial Algeria.

Muqaddam—the man in charge of a quarter of the medina.

Nour—name meaning light.

Oulmès—sparkling mineral water.

Raï —music originating in Algeria, blending traditional and contemporary instruments, the lyrics often dealing with social issues.

Raton—'young rat', a derogatory term used for North Africans in France.

Salam alay-kum—the greeting 'Peace be upon you.'

Salat idh-dhuhr—the noon prayer.

Shukran—'Thank you.'

Shuwafa—a psychic.

Sura—a chapter of the Qur'an.

Tajine—a clay pot with a conical lid for slow-cooking meat and vegetables.

Tuareg—relating to the Berber people of the Saharan interior of North Africa.

Waha—OK.

Wardah—famous Algerian female singer; the name means 'Rose.'